The Submissive Shrew

By

Jane Pearl

Published by Jane Pearl at Smashwords. © 2014, Jane Pearl

ALL RIGHTS RESERVED. This book contains material protected under International and Federal Copyright Laws and Treaties. Any unauthorized reprint or use of this material is prohibited. No part of this book may be reproduced or transmitted in any form or by any means, electronic or mechanical, including photocopying, recording, or by any information storage and retrieval system without express written permission from the author / publisher.

Chapter One – Putting On the Screws

"A dominant husband must always remember that his rules are ultimately in his wife's best interest." Excerpt from How to Be a Dominant Husband by Penelope Wiggins

"Cecelia, I can't believe what a bitch you were tonight!" Stan's fingers tightened on the steering wheel as he expertly navigated the winding drive to their house. He was referring to Cecilia's thinly veiled insults to his co-worker's wives at dinner that evening.

Cecelia held up an elegant, manicured hand and examined the polish. "I don't understand what you're so upset about Stan. They're just your underlings at the bank."

Stan turned his head to glare at her perfect profile. "It doesn't matter who they are. You should treat everyone with respect, no matter what their position in life may be." He turned his attention back to the road and clicked the garage door opener. The black Jaguar slipped into its spot in the garage. Stan could see Cecelia's pearly white twin to his car gleaming in the weak lighting. Turning off the ignition, Stan rotated his body in the seat. "I will put you on notice right now. Such behavior on your part will no longer be accepted. Do you understand?"

His petite wife rolled her eyes. "Whatever Stan. Are you becoming one of those He-Men who thinks he can order his wife around like a serf?" She let off a trill of fake laughter. "I hate to disappoint you but I'm not some 'little woman' running around just itching for the chance to serve you."

Stan's eyes narrowed as his fists clenched in his lap. "We'll see about that." With these ominous words he opened the car door and climbed out. Turning around he leaned down and looked at Cecilia with arctic blue eyes. "I'll be sleeping in the spare bedroom." He turned on his heel and marched out of the garage into the mudroom.

Cecelia sat for a moment with a single wrinkle marring her perfect brow. Then the wrinkle eased and she lifted her shoulders up as if to dismiss her thoughts. Gathering up her wrap and her clutch, Cecelia made her way to the master suite. A smug smile played over her lips as she walked up the staircase. She was certain that Stan would get over his little snit soon and everything would return back to normal. After throwing her fur wrap and clutch onto the delicate chair in the corner of the very feminine bedroom, Cecilia stopped to admire her reflection in the full length mirror on the side of the room. Turning this way and that, she ran her hands over her trim figure closely encased in an expensive grey fine wool dress. Smiling, she raised a hand to the mink brown hair piled on top of her head. Gypsy dark eyes smiled back at her over high cheek bones and full pink lips. The smile widened as she took in the perfect picture she presented. Lifting her nose up in the air, Cecilia gave an indelicate snort. Those bitches tonight just wished they had what she had…a perfect body and a rich older husband who let her do anything she wanted. It was just too bad for them that they didn't manage to snag a catch like her Stan. Satisfied with her conclusions, Cecelia unzipped the dress and started the long beauty routine she indulged in every evening. It was kind of a relief to know that Stan would be sleeping in a guest bedroom tonight. That way, she didn't have to worry about him bugging her for sex!

*****

Cecilia would have been surprised to find out how Stan was actually spending his evening. He'd downloaded a book to his e-reader and, ever the apt student; he was taking notes in a leather bound notebook. Every once in awhile he'd nod his head and smile grimly. Tapping a finger on his chin, he sent up a silent thanks to his friend Joe for suggesting the book to him earlier that night. One thought kept reverberating in his head as he read. It was time for him to curb in his bitchy wife before she ruined his career and their marriage!

*****

The next day, Stan left for his job as a bank president before Cecilia rolled out of bed. Before he left, he placed a note on the kitchen counter for her to read when she finally decided to get up. Adjusting the cuffs of his shirt, he grabbed a long dress coat out of the closet and strolled through the mudroom into the garage.

At around 10 AM Cecelia sauntered into the kitchen. Yawning languidly, she patted a manicured hand over her mouth and walked to the custom individual serving coffee maker on the counter. After placing the coffee pod in the machine and pushing the 'on' button, she pivoted and opened the refrigerator to grab non-fat milk to use as a creamer. She spied the note on the counter as she walked back to the coffee maker to pick up her freshly brewed cup. After dumping some milk into her coffee she place the milk back in the frig and picked up the note on the way to the breakfast nook off of the kitchen. She sat down in the seat next to her closed laptop computer and set her mug on the table. Raising a severely plucked eyebrow she opened Stan's note. "Cecilia, please be home at 6 PM this evening. I have something I must discuss with you." The note was signed with Stan's distinctive slashing signature.

Cecilia pursed her lips and rolled her eyes. Yeah, like she was going to come running when he whistled! Crumpling the note, she opened her laptop and signed in. A coy smile played around her lips as she logged onto Facebook. She had a message! Clicking on the message icon, she read the content. "Hey beautiful…long time no IM. Next time you see me on-line chat me up." Blaine's urbane face appeared in his profile picture on the upper left corner of the message.

Cecilia smiled and responded to his playful banter. "Hey handsome…I'll definitely chat with you next time I'm on FB." She stopped and looked at the time on her computer. "I need to get going right now…have an appointment with my personal trainer, lunch with the girls and then the salon this afternoon. I'll be home tonight though so will definitely keep an eye out for you." She added a winking smiley face icon to the end of her message. Smiling secretively, she closed her laptop and picked up the half finished cup of coffee. Time to work out!

As she walked up to her bedroom to change, she thought about her relationship with Blaine. They'd gone to the same exclusive prep school and had been friends ever since. Recently, their relationship had taken on a new tone when Cecilia started complaining about her husband. Her complaints were all in the same vein…Stan was a fuddy duddy who wanted to stay home and when he did go out, he wanted to go to low brow places like the Salty Dog so he could play pool! This was not the future she'd envisioned when she married him. Knowing how wealthy he was from both his own income and from his family's money, Cecilia had expected they would be going to exclusive events where they would rub elbows with the 'right' people.

Her visions of inspiring lust and envy in the upper crust of society were dashed by Stan's refusal to play along. Blaine, for his part, commiserated with her and complimented her profusely on her beauty. He couldn't understand why Stan didn't treat her like the treasure she was. He assured her that if she were HIS wife, he'd show her off as often as possible. Blaine's statements helped to inflate her already big ego. As a result, she'd started day dreaming about a possible future with Blaine. The only spanner in the works was Blaine's parents who refused to give him any money except for a small stipend. They believed that he should be a self made man rather than a 'trust fund' dilettante. Cecilia knew that there was no way she would be able to support her current lifestyle if she left Stan for Blaine. In five years, though, their pre-nup would be null and void and she'd be able to walk away from Stan with a huge settlement! Though she'd never told Blaine that this was her plan, this exit strategy was rapidly gaining ground as the only possible plan for her future.

Pulling her hair into a bouncy ponytail, Cecilia smiled at the attractive sight she made in her workout clothing. Sitting on a chair in the corner of the room, she tied her tennis shoes then bounced up onto the balls of her feet. Time to work off her liquid breakfast!

The rest of her day went like pretty much any other day in her life. After working out, she showered and dressed to the nines in order to meet her friends for a late lunch. The women she called "friends" were a group of bored wives of rich men whose only entertainment consisted of a round of shopping and gossiping. Cecilia was the acknowledged leader of their group due to her skinny frame and her penchant for vicious gossip. They all sat around the table picking at their salads and sipping sparkling water. In their group, there was a silent competition to see who could consume the least food while appearing to eat. Cecilia usually won and today was no different. She ate one small chunk of chicken, some lettuce, a tomato slice and a carrot. After consuming these items, she pushed her plate away and daintily patted her lips with a cloth napkin. "I am absolutely stuffed!" She looked pointedly at the half empty plate of the woman next to her.

The woman blushed and pushed her plate away. "I'm full too." She hastily declared.

Cecilia gave her an approving nod. "You'll be a size two in no time, Emily, if you keep it up."

Emily, a curvaceous red head, smiled at her eagerly. "I've started eating the way you suggest, Cecilia, and I'm finally losing weight." She frowned. "My husband told me that he liked my curves but I told him that it is difficult to wear couture clothing if you have breasts and hips." She looked at the group triumphantly. "He's quit grumbling about it. I know he's going to love it when I actually reach a size two…I mean what man wouldn't like a fashionably thin wife?" All of the skeletally thin women around the table nodded sagely at her words.

Cecilia raised a glass of sparkling water. "Here's to Emily."

All of the women responded. "Hear, hear!" Emily blushed again and glowed with pride at their words.

After lunch, Cecilia and a few of her friends went shopping in the couture shops next to the restaurant. After shopping all afternoon, Cecilia excused herself to go to her salon. She rushed through the salon door at 5:45 PM, just in time for her appointment with the manicurist. "Sally darling, I just need a quick fill and a new color." The Asian woman nodded and quietly set to work. Around 6:00 PM her cell phone vibrated to indicate a text. Cecilia shrugged. Whoever it was would just have to wait. She couldn't pick up the phone until her nails had dried. Sally finished about thirty minutes later and led Cecilia to the hardening station. Cecilia slid her hands under the blue lights and waited the required amount of time. After drying her nails, she picked up the phone and checked her texts.

It was from Stan. "I told you that I wanted you to be here when I got home at 6:00 PM. Where are you?"

Cecilia shrugged and answered him. "I had a nail appointment that I couldn't miss. I'll be home soon."

His answer came back almost immediately. "Good, I really need to talk to you."

Cecilia took her time going home. She stopped at a gourmet takeout restaurant and picked up dinner for herself and Stan. She smiled as she loaded the warm bags into her pearly white Jaguar.

This should help to appease Stan. She got home at 7:30 PM and walked into the kitchen bearing the white takeout bags. "Stan, I'm home." She called out as she unloaded the food. After a few minutes, Stan appeared in the doorway between the kitchen and the dining room. He hadn't changed from his work clothing though he'd removed his suit jacket and his tie. His light blonde hair stood up from his head as if he'd run his fingers through it repeatedly. He'd rolled up his sleeves to expose hairy muscular forearms. Cecelia noted that he held a sheaf of white papers in his left hand. He gestured towards the living room with his other hand.

"Cecilia, leave the food. We need to talk."

With a frown between her eyebrows Cecilia set the food on the island in the center of the kitchen and trailed behind him. "Sit there." Stan indicated a large chair in the seating group in the living room. Looking at him with a perplexed frown, Cecilia complied. She sat on the chair and folded her arms over her chest. Her body language radiated impatience and anger.

"So what is so important that you felt the need to order me around like a subordinate?" Her jaw jutted out stubbornly.

Stan stopped himself as he started to sit down in the chair opposite hers. He fixed her with an icy blue stare. "Watch your attitude Cecilia. I'm already pretty pissed off right now without you making it worse." He sat down heavily in the chair while placing the papers on the coffee table in front of him.

He cleared his throat. "Cecilia, after last night I realized that we need to make some changes in our marriage." He leaned forward with his elbows resting on his knees and his hands loosely clasped together. He looked down for a moment and then looked up at her. "I've been concerned for some time at the way your treat other people." He took a deep breath. "And how you take care of yourself. I mean look at you." He swept a hand out towards her. "You're painfully thin…you know that the doctor said you wouldn't be able to have children if you didn't gain some weight. "

Cecilia frowned at him and crossed her legs. The top leg started to jiggle angrily on the bottom one. She clenched her lips together until they were just a straight line. "So where are you going with all of this Stan?"

He made a hushing sound. "I'm not done yet." He pulled a piece of paper out of the pile and handed it to her. "Here's your credit card statement for the last month. I've highlighted the charges by category; personal training, eating out, beauty treatments and shopping." He took another breath. "As you can see, the total you spent in one month could fund a small country for a year." He caught her eyes in a steady gaze. "This has all got to stop if you want to remain married to me."

Cecilia dropped her arms down to her sides where her hands clenched into fists. She sat up straight and looked at him in fury. "Are you threatening me with divorce?"

Stan kept looking her in the eyes while pulling another sheaf of papers out of the pile. "You may recognize this darling. It's our pre-nuptial agreement." He handed it to her. "Note the clause concerning the year of marriage when this agreement will be null and void and you will be able to take a sizeable settlement if we divorce. " He cleared his throat again. "We've been married five years…you can't touch any of my assets except for a small payoff if we divorce before we've been married ten years."

Cecilia nodded slowly. She already knew this fact and was even making plans to escape after the five years were up! Looking at Stan warily she glanced down at the pre-nup then looked back up into his intent light blue eyes. "So…where do we go from here?"

Stan smiled triumphantly. He was ready to close the deal. "If you want to remain married to me, you are going to have to start submitting to some rules I've set up." He paused to pull another piece of paper out of the pile. "Here they are." He handed the sheet to her. "If you break my rules there will be repercussions."

Cecilia broke in. "Repercussions? Like what…I'll be grounded?" This came out snottily as she folded her arms again.

Stan shook his head slowly. "No, more like spankings with either my bare hand or an implement of some sort. As a submissive wife you will bow to my will or else."

Cecilia stood up in outrage. The papers piled in her lap fell to the floor in a rush. Her face turned bright red and her fists clenched again. "You have to be kidding me!"

Stan shook his head again this time with a rueful smile. "Nope. I've let you run unchecked for too long and I plan to remedy that situation." He paused. "So, I need your answer right now. Are you ready to continue this marriage under my rule or do you want to go your own way?" He waited for her answer with baited breath.

Cecilia wrapped her arms around her middle and turned so her back was to him. She thought furiously about her options. If she left Stan now, she'd have wasted five of her prime years. If she put up with his silly demands, she could walk away with half of his fortune five years from now and go to Blaine with enough money for them to do whatever they wanted. Coming to a decision, she turned back to face Stan. "I'll accede to your demands."

Stan walked to stand by her and picked up a sheet of paper. "You had better read this before you agree to my dominion." He handed her the list.

Cecilia started to read the list. "Number One, Cecilia will have sex with Stan anytime he wants without complaint. No part of her body is off limits." She rolled her eyes. Whatever! She continued to read out loud. "Number Two, Cecilia will treat everyone with politeness and respect." She'd expected that one after their argument the night before. "Number Three, Cecilia will gain ten pounds in order to improve her chances of conceiving naturally." Yeah right she would. She continued reading. "Exercise will be limited to three one hour sessions a week in order to reach this goal." We will see about that! "Number Four, Cecilia will eat most of her meals at home. She will cook and serve Stan breakfast, lunch and dinner." God, he wanted a Suzy homemaker! "Number Five, In order to accomplish Rule Four Cecilia will need to take cooking lessons." OMG...he had to be kidding. "Number Six, Cecilia must learn to keep to a budget for shopping and personal care." Stan had listed a respectable amount of money as her monthly budget. Unfortunately, Cecilia usually spent twice that amount! She kept reading. "Number Seven, Cecilia will limit her computer use to one hour a day."

Stan broke in and commented. "I've noticed that you've been spending a lot of time on your laptop recently. I want us to spend more time together so thought that limiting your computer use would help to accomplish that goal."

Cecilia glared at him and looked back down at the list. She'd just use the computer while he was at work. She continued reading. "Number Eight, Cecilia must do volunteer work at least three days a week, preferably with children." She quirked an eyebrow at Stan in askance.

He hastened to explain. "I've heard that being around children can help women conceive if they are having difficulty."

Cecilia dropped her head back down to look at the list and rolled her eyes before reading on. "Number Nine, Cecilia must learn a domestic hobby for evenings since she won't be spending all of her time on her laptop." She dropped the list to her lap and attempted to maintain control of her increasingly fragile composure. "So you must have visions of your 'pioneer' wife cooking for you and doing handwork in the evenings." She swept a hand to indicate their surroundings. "I'm surprised that you haven't put our house up for sale so we can move out to a farm in the country. That way you could keep me barefoot and pregnant all of the time!"

Stan surprised her by laughing. "Don't tempt me darling. I like the mental picture you've just painted." His eyes darkened as they swept up and down her form. Cecilia recoiled in horror. Her rich sophisticated husband actually wanted her to become the "little woman" taking care of him and their future children! She'd always envisioned a future of housekeepers and nannies while she continued with her current busy schedule. She was rapidly seeing this future fade away. Thoughts ran through her head furiously. An urge to just walk away from Stan's expectations warred with her greed. Various scenarios ran through her head. Unfortunately, in all cases Stan held all of the cards if she wanted a large divorce settlement.

Finally, Cecilia's shoulders slumped in acceptance. "So what happens now?" Her voice was so low, Stan strained to hear it.

Stan stood up and held out a hand to her. "Now we start implementing the rules." A puzzled Cecilia held a hand up to him and allowed him to pull her to standing. He led her to an armless chair in the corner of the room and sat down. "You've earned a disciplinary spanking for not coming home when I told you to. I want you to pull up your dress, pull down your underwear and lie across my lap."

Cecilia's eyes opened wide in outrage. "You're going to spank me like a child?"

Stan looked up at her with implacable eyes. "If you act like a child, I will treat you like one. Now do as I say or I will increase the punishment by five spanks." He patted his lap and looked at her expectantly.

Suddenly flushed with humiliation, Cecilia wiggled as she pulled the tight skirt of her dress up to her waist. She delicately shimmied a miniscule thong down over her hips. Stan stopped her from taking them off completely. "Leave them at your knees. Now lie across my lap." Cecilia awkwardly complied by settling herself over his hard thighs. She stabilized herself with hands spread wide on the carpet. The toes of her super high heels barely grazed the carpet on the other side. The underwear kept her from spreading her legs wider. She stiffened as she felt Stan's heavy hand press on the small of her back. Surprisingly, she could feel her pussy start to swell and weep at the situation.

Stan took in the beauty laid out before him. Cecilia's elegantly coiffed hair looked incongruous considering the fact that she was over his lap with her couture dress rucked up to her waist. He ran an appreciative hand over the smooth white flesh of her buttocks. Though she was too thin, her rear stood out pertly from compulsive exercising. Stan continued to caress her, running a hand down the back of her leg to the delicate scrap of material bisecting her thighs then back up her inner thigh. Stan raised his eyebrows in surprise when he encountered moisture on her bare pussy. Something about this situation made his shrewish wife cream! He'd definitely have to pursue this line of inquiry further.

Finally, he lifted his heavy hand and brought it down hard on his wife's right buttock. Smack! Both he and Cecilia started at the noise. Wasting little time, he brought it down on her left buttock. Smack! Now both of her butt cheeks had angry red palm marks that stood out starkly against Cecilia's pearly white flesh. Smack! Smack! Smack! Stan laid into her ass with a flurry of spanks. Cecilia started moaning and squirming on his lap. She reached a hand back as if to cover herself. Stan grabbed her wrist and pinned it over the small of her back. "Don't cover yourself or I'll add to your punishment." He noticed that his wife's color was high and she had begun to breathe rapidly. She'd also started to rapidly blink her eyes as if to keep back tears. To finish the punishment, Stan peppered her ass and thighs with his hardest spanks. He was gratified to see tears spring in Cecilia's eyes and begin to roll down her cheeks. He soothingly rubbed her butt while she sobbed silently. "I think that your disrespect merits some corner time." He pointed to a corner next to their dining room table. "I want you to stand there with your skirt held up and your underwear down by your knees while I eat this dinner you've picked up for us." With Stan's help, Cecilia pushed herself up to standing and shuffled over to the indicated corner with her couture dress held high at her waist. Though she'd just been admonished, she held her head with a regal air as if her bright red ass weren't on display above long luscious legs ending in sky high couture shoes. Stan walked into the kitchen and helped himself to the food his wife had brought home. He carried the plate into the dining room and sat in a seat that afforded him good view of her figure in the corner. He could occasionally see her shoulders shudder as she sobbed. His cock stiffened at the thought of how wet her pussy had become during the spanking. It seemed that Joe was right. Spanking did enhance sexual pleasure. He couldn't wait to find out this evening!

Finishing up his meal, he walked into the kitchen and rinsed his plate. Filling a clean plate, he walked into the dining room and set it on the table. Looking over at Cecilia, he cleared his throat then spoke. "Uh, you can pull up your panties up and your dress down. When you're done, come over to me." His wife did as he instructed and came to stand by him. Though she attempted to hide it, her eyes held a hint of defiance over flushed cheeks. Stan grabbed her hand and pulled her down to sit draped over his lap. He wrapped a supportive hand around her back while tenderly wiping the tears from her cheeks with a cloth napkin. "I'm sorry that I had to do that sweetheart." He smiled into her watery dark brown eyes. "Do you understand why you got a spanking?"

Cecilia's jaw firmed and anger flashed through her eyes. She didn't answer his question. Instead, she mutinously lowered her head and tucked it on his shoulder. Stan lifted her chin with a finger and sternly gazed into her eyes. "Answer me wife or you'll earn another ten." His hand slipped down to rub over her hot posterior.

Cecilia's eyes opened in alarm. "I didn't come home when you told me to." She hastily answered.

Stan nodded his head with gravity. "That is correct...Do you have something to say to me in regards to this infraction?"

A frown marred Cecilia's brow. "Uh, I'm sorry?"

"For..." Stan prompted.

Cecilia swallowed and then continued. "I'm sorry for not coming home when you told me to."

Stan's hand started to pet her head where it rested on his shoulder. "Good girl. Now you can eat some dinner." He picked up a fork and took a healthy portion of food from the plate. "Open up!" Cecilia looked at him in horror. He was going to feed her? The amount on the fork was about half of what she'd normally allow herself to consume for the evening meal. Knowing that he'd brook no arguments, Cecilia delicately took a small bite from the fork. Stan watched her attempt to eat as little as possible with a smirk on his face. Holding the fork in front of her face, he firmly stated. "I expect you to eat everything on this plate so you might as well get on with it."

Cecilia reared back in his arms and looked at him aghast. "I can't eat that much!"

Stan smiled at her smugly. "How else are you going to be able to gain ten pounds?"

Cecilia crossed her arms angrily over her chest. Her whole body radiated rebellion. "You have got to be kidding."

A warning light entered Stan's eyes. "Do we need to go over the rules again my dear?"

Cecilia shifted gingerly on his lap. Her aching buttocks reminded her of who held the control in their relationship now. She opened her lips in resignation and took the whole bite off of the fork.

Chapter Two – Mixed Results

"Once you've established the rules for your wife, you may experience an initial rocky patch followed by an increasing sense of marital accord." Excerpt from How to Be a Dominant Husband by Penelope Wiggins

The next morning, Cecilia walked around the kitchen with her butt twitching angrily like a pissed off cat. She fumed as she cleaned up the dishes from their breakfast. Their breakfast…hah! This morning Stan had woken her with a rough shake on her hip. When she refused to move, he slapped her hard on the ass. "Get up wife. It's time for you to make me breakfast."

Cecilia rolled over on her back and blinked at him slowly like an owl. "What time is it?" Her voice came out in a croak.

"6:00 AM…come on let's go." He pulled the covers off of her and pulled her reluctant form up to a sitting position. He turned her so she was sitting on the side of the bed. He gently placed slippers on her feet and helped her stand. "Here's your robe." He wrapped a fluffy peignoir around her, covering a sheer designer baby doll nightgown. Cecilia placed a delicate hand over her mouth as she yawned. Stan smiled and wrapped his arm around her shoulders. "In case you forgot, the kitchen is this way."

Cecilia fumed as she threw a wet sponge into the sink. She thought back on the morning spent with her loving husband. Loving…hah! He'd ordered her to make breakfast for him and when she'd refused he'd flipped up the frilly edge of her short nightie and firmly smacked her already sore ass with a spatula. Finally, she'd relented and stomped around while putting together a paltry breakfast of cereal, fruit and coffee. Stan was all smiles as she served him. "Now you need to make something for yourself and eat it." Cecilia grabbed a mug and quickly made her usual breakfast of coffee and non-fat milk. Stan raised his eyebrows when she sat down next to him and started sipping from the mug. "There's no way that is enough for breakfast." He commented. "I want to see you eat something more substantial." After giving him a sideways look, she sighed and got up to open the refrigerator. Her eyes lit on a container of non-fat yogurt. That should appease him. Grabbing the container and a spoon, she sat down and started to eat with dramatic flare. Stan nodded approvingly and tucked into his own meal.

After breakfast, Stan laid down the law as far as her approved activities for the day. Handing her a small hard back book, he said. "Your assignment for today is to start reading this book and design a meal plan for the week. I've placed a word document on the desktop of your laptop with a list of my favorite foods. I also gave you a word document of my favorite childhood recipes."

Cecilia frowned at him. "When did you do that?"

He smiled at her like a cat that ate the canary. "After you fell asleep last night." Cecilia blushed and dropped her head. After Stan had finished feeding her, he'd carried her into the bedroom where he'd made passionate love to her. Cecilia had been so responsive after his discipline, she'd come repeatedly during their interlude. Stan must have gotten back up after she'd fallen into an exhausted slumber. Stan continued speaking. "I also placed spyware on your laptop so I will know where you've been cruising on the internet."

Cecilia's eyes widened in outrage. "What!"

Stan took a deep drink of his coffee. "I know that you'll need the internet to research some of the assignments I've given you as part of the rules I've set down. I don't want you to waste any of your time while on the computer. You need to get in, get the information and get out."

Cecilia fisted her hands in the frothy hem of her robe. "I can't even check e-mails or Facebook?"

Stan shook his head. "No, that can wait until the evening when I get home." He paused. "I've also put a tracker on your smart phone. I'll know if you've been roaming on it as well."

Tears welled in Cecilia's eyes. "Don't you trust me?"

Stan stopped and looked her in the eyes. "I feel like you haven't been making the best choices in recent years. You waste your time with frivolous activities and with friends who are incredibly shallow." He ran a hand through his hair. "I'm tired of seeing you fall further and further into a life of mindless pursuits." Seeing the tears spill down her cheeks, he pulled her close in his arms.

Wrapping one hand around her waist while stroking the tumbled brown hair on her head with the other, he spoke softly in her ear. "I know you are more than what you appear to be. That's why I chose you to be my wife and....the mother of my children." He softly kissed her ear. "I love you. There is no other reason I'd go to all of this trouble." Cecilia's sobs dwindled as she rocked in his arms. Stan pushed her away from him while he wiped the tears from her cheeks with his thumb. "Now I want you to go shopping for this week's food and start searching for volunteer opportunities, cooking and hobby classes. I have some ideas about volunteering if you come up empty on that search." He kissed her on the forehead. "I'll be home for lunch. You don't have to serve me anything elaborate, just a soup and sandwich are fine." He walked towards the door to the mudroom and then stopped for a moment and turned to face her again. "Call your personal trainer and tell him you'll only be seeing him three days a week from now on." He glanced at his watch and started to exit the room once again. "I'll see you at noon darling. Oh, and start reading that book. I expect you to finish it this week." This was thrown over his shoulder as he closed the mudroom door.

    Realizing that she only had so much time until lunch, Cecilia hurried to grab her laptop and open it. Per Stan's instructions there were two word documents on the desktop. One was titled "Stan's favorite foods" and the other was titled "Stan's favorite childhood recipes". Cecilia hurriedly opened both documents and set up a bare bones food plan for the week. After printing her shopping list, she ran up the stairs to her bedroom and showered quickly before leaving the house to go grocery shopping. Returning home three hours later, Cecilia unloaded all of her purchases into the spacious freezer in the pantry and onto the pantry shelves. She'd already decided to serve Stan a good canned soup and a simple meat and cheese sandwich. Looking at the clock, she realized that she didn't have much time until he came home for lunch! She was just finishing cutting his sandwiches when she heard the door to the mudroom open, heralding Stan's arrival. She nervously rubbed her hands on the apron she'd thrown over her designer jeans and sweater ensemble. Stan sauntered into the kitchen with his nose raised in the air obviously smelling the food she'd prepared. "Mmm...smells good!" He dropped a kiss on her nose before pulling out a chair at the breakfast bar on the far side of the kitchen island.

Feeling stupidly nervous, Cecilia brought him the plate of sandwiches and ran to the stove to serve him a bowl of soup. Setting the bowl and a soup spoon in front of him, she stood next to him with her hands nervously wrapped around her waist. Stan gave her a quick sideways glance and blew on the hot soup in his spoon. "You need to serve yourself some soup and at least half a sandwich honey." Some of Cecilia's former attitude made an appearance as she stomped to the stove and filled a small cup half full with soup. She continued to stomp as she grabbed a small half sandwich off of the full plate and placed it on a small dish next to the soup bowl. Sitting down in the empty seat at the breakfast bar with an aggrieved sigh, she began to pick at her food in her usual fashion. Stan glanced at her with a brief smile before returning to his meal. "I want you to eat all of it honey. If you've gained a little weight at tomorrow's weigh-in I'll reward you with an orgasm." With these words he bent his head to sip some soup off of his spoon.

Oh…my…fucking …god…he actually is going to control my pleasure in order to make me gain weight! These words reverberated through Cecilia's head as she dutifully sipped her soup and ate the sandwich. She shifted uncomfortably on the saddle seat of the bar height chair. Her buttocks were still hot and sore from the spankings she'd received in the last two days. For some reason, her discomfort lit a fire in her clit. She really would like him to fuck her again before he went back to work. She glanced at Stan out of the corner of her eyes. Maybe she'd get a few orgasms today before he cut her off tomorrow. After all, there was no way she'd agree to gain ten pounds! After finishing the last bit of her food, Cecilia seductively stood up and leaned over Stan to take his plate and bowl. Looking into his eyes meaningfully she breathed. "Is there anything else I can do for you today…husband?"

Stan's eyes bored into hers and as he took in her jean clad form. "I would normally want to fuck you but since you're wearing pants I guess I'll just settle for a blow job."

Cecilia recoiled as his words hit her. "Okay…just let me put these dishes away." She sashayed to the dishwasher and placed their dishes in the machine. Leaning over the dishwasher, she glanced at Stan over her shoulder. "Are you sure you wouldn't want more than a BJ?"

He smiled and unzipped his pants. "It shouldn't take very long."

Cecilia dragged her feet as she came to stand by his side. Twisting her hair in one hand, she placed it under the neck of her sweater. Looking up at Stan lasciviously, she licked her lips and pulled his cock out of his pants. Oh…it was a monster! Sometimes she forgot. Licking her lips she dropped her lipstick encrusted mouth to the top of the bulbous purple tip. Looking up at her husband with velvety brown eyes, she quickly engulfed his tool right down to the root. Stan moaned and grabbed her head as she started to rapidly work her mouth and throat up and down its thick length. She felt his cock start to lengthen as he reached his climax. Stan took over right before he came and fucked his cock deep into her oral cavity until he climaxed in great pulsing streams…right down her throat. Cecilia attempted to swallow all he gave her and remained quiescent until he was done. Stan gently removed his penis from her mouth when he was done and dropped a kiss to the top of her head. "Thanks babe. That was a great nooner."

Cecilia blinked her eyes and returned to a standing posture. "Uh, I'm glad you liked it. I'll see you tonight when you get home from work." She blindly turned to grab the cleaning sponge from the sink. She frenetically cleaned the crumbs off of the countertop as Stan left for work. After she heard the door to the garage close, she threw the sponge into the sink. This situation sucked so much! So he got to come but she didn't? So unfair… She paced around the kitchen with her arms wrapped around her middle. Oh crap…she needed to do some internet research and figure out what was for dinner tonight. Rubbing her sore behind, she ran to her laptop.

*****

That evening, Stan came home to the wonderful aroma of home cooking. As he walked through the kitchen, he took a peek in the oven to see a meatloaf baking in one pan with another foil covered pan. From the odor, he assumed that it contained carrots and potatoes. Yum! He walked through the kitchen to the living room. Cecilia sat on the couch with book he'd given her that morning on her lap. Her brow wrinkled as she read the marital manual. "Hello darling…" Stan caroled as he walked into the room. "Dinner smells delicious." He leaned over to drop a kiss on her head. Cecilia absently smiled and waved in his direction. "I'll be down in a bit for dinner." He advised her as he exited the room.

When he came downstairs, the dining room table was set with two place settings and candles. Cecilia waited by the table dressed in a knee length dress, pearls and heels. "Dinner is served."

Stan dropped a kiss on her mouth and took a seat at the table. "Looks fantastic darling!" Cecilia smiled at him and hurried to serve dinner.

After dinner, Stan and Cecilia retired to the media room. Stan sat on the couch watching television while Cecilia sat in one of the armchairs taking advantage of her free hour on the computer. She logged into Facebook and saw that there were several messages waiting for her. Glancing sideways at Stan, she clicked on the message icon. All of the messages were from Blaine getting increasingly frantic. Clicking on the last message, she typed in a brief reply. "Husband is cracking down on computer time. I'll message you when I can." She added a smiley face icon to let Blaine know that everything was okay. Chancing a brief glare up at Stan, she scrolled through the Newsfeed from her friends. Occasionally she slowed down to look at pictures of her friend's kids. Without realizing it, she gave a big sigh.

Stan glanced at her and his forehead wrinkled. "Are you okay Hon?"

Pasting on a smile, Cecilia nodded and wrapped up her computer time. Stan crooked a finger at her, signaling her to come join him on the sofa. Placing the computer on a side table, she took a seat next to her husband. Stan wrapped an arm around her shoulder. Cecilia awkwardly attempted to relax in his embrace but had difficulty letting go enough to rest against him. Finally, she folded her legs to one side and slid stiffly under his arm. Stan frowned at her briefly then tightened his grip. Feeling like a hostage, Cecilia endured his touch until it was time for bed. She breathed a sigh of relief when Stan released her. "Go on up to bed Hon. I'll be there soon." Stan stood and stretched then offered her a hand up. Cecilia gladly escaped his company and hurried upstairs in order to get ready for bed.

That night Stan woke Cecilia up for sex when he came to bed. She gave in to his demands immediately but had difficulty climaxing. Finally she faked an orgasm by moaning loudly and clenching her vaginal muscles. Stan immediately came with a shout, releasing a hot rush of cum into her vagina. After he'd withdrawn, Cecilia immediately attempted to go to the bathroom so she could clean up. Stan drew her tightly into his arms and wouldn't let her go. "You aren't allowed to wash off my seed anymore. I want to know that you carry my cum inside you after we've made love." They fell asleep spoon style with Stan's hand cupped possessively over her bare pussy.

*****

Over the following week, Cecilia found a cooking school and was able to sign up for an embroidery class at a local craft store. Her search for a volunteer opportunity didn't go as well. She finally asked Stan where he thought she should go. He gave her the name and phone number of a business in a part of the town Cecilia would describe as being on the wrong side of the tracks. Cecilia was surprised at how nervous she was when she called the place to set an appointment to talk to the director. Stacy, the director, was incredibly friendly and enthusiastic about an additional volunteer. She quickly set up an appointment with Cecilia for the next morning.

After serving Stan breakfast the next day, Cecilia nervously prepared for the meeting. She stuck her tongue out at her reflection in the mirror while applying makeup. Why was she so worried about meeting the director of some low budget non-profit? She haughtily ran her hands down the sides of her expensive sweater dress. It probably cost more than the director made in a month! She finished off her outfit with cable knit tights tucked into expensive leather high heeled boots. She'd opted for a simple ponytail in an attempt to dress down. Walking downstairs, she grabbed her purse and a long leather coat with a large fur ruff.

Cecilia wrinkled her nose in distaste as she parked her Jaguar in the parking lot of a dilapidated building smack dab in the middle of the worst neighborhood in town. She looked around apprehensively at the poorly maintained parking lot and decrepit buildings as well as the numerous homeless people loitering on the street. Taking a deep breath she turned off the engine and climbed out of the low slung car. Pointing her key fob at the vehicle, she locked the doors then placed the keys carefully in her purse. Hugging the purse tightly under her arm, she walked rapidly around the corner to the entrance of the building. As she neared the front door, she noted the name of the business emblazoned on the front window, "Tiny Sprouts Day Care and Pre-school". A day care! What the hell. She stopped and took another deep breath before opening the door. As she opened the door, her senses were instantly assaulted with the noise created by children playing and an underlying odor of food with a whiff of something that smelled like poop. Ugh…diapers! She shuddered at the thought. She looked around to see if she could identify an authority figure. Since no one came up to her, she finally walked up to a petite blond woman dressed in a long sleeved t-shirt and jeans helping a tiny girl finish a coloring activity. "Excuse me miss…I'm here to meet with Stacy?" The blond looked up at her from a crouch by the child's side. Her expressive blue eyes took in Cecilia's high-end apparel before she rose up to greet her.

Wiping her hand on the front of her jeans, the woman offered Cecilia a hand. "Hi, I'm Stacy. It's nice to meet you." Cecilia hesitated to shake her hand, wondering if she'd recently changed a baby. She repressed an internal shudder at the thought and offered her hand to Stacy. As they shook, Cecilia compared her hand to the program director's hand. Cecilia's hand was obviously manicured with fake nails and expensive rings. Stacy's hand had no nonsense short nails, one simple gold band on her ring finger and no polish. Her skin was slightly rough as if she washed it frequently. Looking around at the children, Cecilia could understand why she'd feel the need to avoid contagion.

Stacy dropped Cecilia's hand and gestured towards a group of chairs in the corner of the room. "Let's go over there and talk." They picked their way through the energetic toddlers and sat facing each other in the quiet corner. Stacy took a deep breath and looked Cecilia up and down again. Slapping her hands on her thighs she started to speak. "So…" She paused for a moment. "You would like to volunteer with us?" Her voice lilted up lightly at the end of the statement as if it were a question.

Cecilia nodded hesitantly. "Yes, I think that it is time that I gave back to the community and Stan, my husband, mentioned your agency." She looked around. "I didn't realize that it was a daycare."

Stacy looked intrigued. "Stan…Stan Bergstrom?"

Cecilia started with surprise. "Yes, you know him?"

Stacy smiled warmly. "He's friends with my husband, Carl Westin."

A bulb went on in Cecilia's brain. She vaguely remembered Stan mentioning an old friend named Carl. He'd wanted the two couples to get together but Cecilia hadn't been interested. She didn't want to socialize with people who didn't move in the right circles. It was bad enough that Stan forced her to associate with his employees! Dismissing her internal dialogue, Cecilia smiled insincerely and nodded. "Oh, of course, Carl! I remember Stan mentioning him."

Stacy looked at her oddly. "They meet every week to play golf at the Country Club. I'm surprised we haven't met before now."

Cecilia nodded and acted perplexed. "Me too. Well, I guess there's no time like the present." She blinked rapidly and kept the smile pasted to her face.

Stacy looked at her another moment then seemed to do a mental shrug. She also pasted a fake smile on her face. "So, you want to volunteer at Tiny Sprouts. Do you have any idea of what you'd like to do here?"

Cecilia shrugged. "I'm not really sure. I don't have any experience with child care. Is there anything else you need to have done?"

Stacy paused for a moment as if to gather her thoughts. "First of all, I should really tell you what our program is about." She crossed her legs and laced her fingers around the top knee. "Tiny Sprouts is a daycare and pre-school program for children of the working poor." She shifted in her seat. "Most of their parents would be on welfare if it weren't for our program. Once they factor in the cost of child care, their take home pay ends up being a fraction of their hourly wage so many of them just give up and get on the dole." She coughed into her hand then resumed her grasp on the knee. "About ten years ago, my husband's family decided to form Tiny Sprouts in conjunction with a vocational training program. This program helps undertrained workers who can only get minimum wage jobs. Once they are done with their area of study, they are also given help in order to obtain a job in their specialty." She smiled happily. "Little Sprouts provides daycare and pre-school for the children of program participants until they can afford the price of regular childcare." She smiled sheepishly. "As far as help other than childcare, I really could use some organizational expertise in my office." She leaned forward to whisper conspiratorially. "I really hate paperwork."

Cecilia smiled at her in relief. "I can totally do that!" She held out her hand to Stacy who shook it in bemusement.

"So, what days and times can you help?" Stacy inquired.

"Uh, I'm planning on three afternoons a week if that is okay? Cecilia asked.

Stacy stood up and offered her hand. "Perfect! I'll see you starting Monday at 2:00PM. Is Monday, Wednesday and Friday all right with you?"

Cecilia nodded her head. "Great." She stood as well and took Stacy's hand. "I'll see you on Monday." Looking around like she'd dodged a bullet; Cecilia picked her way through the children to the front door. Escaping into the fresh air she hurried towards her car and punched the key fob.

*****

Over the weekend, Stan decided to institute a daily maintenance spanking for Cecilia. After observing her through the first week under his rule, he realized that she was much more eager for sex when she'd been recently spanked. He suspected that she'd faked orgasms with him on more than one occasion in the last week and, in fact, throughout their five year marriage. He wanted to be able to allow or deny the real thing as a means to control her, especially in relation to weight gain. Much to his delight and Cecelia's chagrin she attempted to cajole him into fucking her throughout the day after a spanking. If she'd gained weight, he'd allow at least one orgasm per day. If her weight stayed the same or if she'd lost weight, he'd take his pleasure of her body but wouldn't allow her to come. This policy along with the humiliation of her own need drove Cecilia crazy.

*****

The second week into their arrangement, they settled into a new daily routine. Every morning, Stan woke Cecelia up and ordered her over his lap for a brisk spanking. Since the spanking was meant to be more of a reminder rather than a punishment, he kept his slaps light. In order to prime Cecilia's arousal, he liked to take small breaks between spanks to lightly caress her sodden pussy. For her part, Cecelia resented his power over her body. She didn't want to want him but couldn't seem to help herself after a spanking. After administering her maintenance spanking, Stan flipped down her nightgown and helped her to her feet. Their next stop was the bathroom where Cecelia was allowed to urinate before her weigh-in. Stan kept a card in the vanity drawer upon which he recorded her morning weight. Cecelia was appalled to realize that she'd gained three pounds in the seven days since they started their agreement. Some of her tighter clothing was already feeling too small!

The next order of business was a breakfast prepared by Cecilia then Stan left for work after kissing Cecilia on the head. On Monday, Wednesday and Friday she worked out with her personal trainer in the morning and then prepared lunch for Stan and herself. Some days she served Stan at home and some days she took a sack lunch to his office. After lunch she reported to Tiny Sprouts to volunteer.

Tuesday and Thursday mornings were spent either at the cooking school or at the craft store. To her surprise, Cecilia enjoyed learning domestic skills. Tuesday and Thursday afternoon were spent reading the marital manual Stan had provided called How to Be a Submissive Wife and cruising the internet for new recipes.

On the Friday of the second week of their arrangement, she took lunch to Joe's office and happened to run into Sarah, the wife of one of Stan's vice presidents at the bank. Cecilia attempted to smooth her obviously rumpled hair. Stan had grabbed it with both hands while he fucked her mouth after lunch.

"Hello Cecilia. What brings you to the office during the day?" Sarah looked at her curiously.

Cecilia blushed and said, "Stan wanted me to bring him lunch today…so I just dropped it off."

"Hmmm…." Sarah looked at her in amazement. "I didn't know that you do such errands for him."

Cecilia glanced down and then up at Sarah through her lashes. "I didn't used to but Stan has been making…demands of me…changes in my behavior…and if I don't comply there are…consequences."

Comprehension dawned on Sarah's face. "So he really did it!" Grabbing Cecilia's elbow Sarah said. "Walk with me so we can talk." An unusually subdued Cecilia nodded her head and accompanied Sarah down the hallway.

"So, did he give you How to Be a Submissive Wife?" Cecilia shot her a surprised glance and then looked down and nodded sharply. "Are you reading it?" Again Cecilia nodded. Sarah placed her hand on Cecilia's arm in compassion. "Do you have any questions? Joe and I have been in a Domestic Discipline marriage for a few months now so I am pretty experienced in these matters."

Cecilia started to talk and then stopped. "So…do you find that you are actually turned on by being disciplined?" Her cheeks blazed bright red with this question.

"Yes, since we've started this way of life I'm wet most of the time." Sarah smiled sheepishly. "Good thing too since Joe enjoys playing with my body throughout the day. Why do you think he had me bring his lunch to the office today? He doesn't like to miss his lunchtime play session." With these words, Sarah rolled her eyes.

Cecilia looked relieved. "Does Joe let you come?"

"Most of the time, unless I'm being punished. He doesn't allow any orgasms outside of his presence though." Sarah replied.

Cecelia looked frustrated. "Stan is only allowing me a few orgasms a week though he gets to come once or twice a day." She sputtered. "It isn't fair!"

"Does he say why he is limiting your orgasms?" Sarah inquired.

"He says that he is looking for certain behavioral and physical changes before he will allow me to come more often."

"Like what?" Sarah's brow furrowed.

Cecelia's cheeks pinked up again. "He wants me to gain some weight. He says that he doesn't like fucking a bag of bones. He's limited me to exercising only three days a week and I have to eat regular meals. I've already gained three pounds!"

Sarah looked her up and down. "How much does he want you to gain?"

"About ten pounds. I've had irregular periods for years and the doctor says it is because I am too thin. We want to have children so

Stan has decided that if I have more body fat our chances of conceiving will increase."

Sarah's face softened. "It sounds like Stan has your best interests at heart." She smiled at Cecilia. "In order to succeed in a Domestic Discipline marriage you need to have faith in your husband's judgment about what is best for you. Once you surrender yourself to his will, you will reap limitless rewards." She stopped walking and reached into her purse. Writing a number on a slip of paper, she handed it to Cecilia. "If you need someone to talk to or a shoulder to cry on, give me a call. Maybe we should see if we can set up a group of submissive wives to talk about our struggles in surrendering to our husband's will."

Cecilia's face brightened. "I would love that!" Then sobering she turned to look at Sarah in the face. "I need to apologize to you for being such a bitch all of these years. Stan has shown me the error of my ways." She ruefully rubbed her behind with these words. "He has promised me that the punishment will be immediate if he sees any sort of bitchiness on my part to anyone. I'm a little afraid for the employee Christmas party. This will be my first time attending such a function as a submissive wife."

Sarah patted her shoulder. "I'm sure you will do fine. Put yourself in Stan's hands and all will be well." With these words, Sarah pulled her key chain out of her purse and opened her car door. "I'll see you this weekend at the office Christmas party!"

Cecilia waved at her as she drove away. It was nice to know that someone else was in the same boat as her. Shaking her head, she walked over to her car. It was time to volunteer at the daycare…sigh.

*****

Cecilia gazed at her reflection apprehensively as she prepared for the office Christmas party. Knowing that Stan expected her on her best behavior, she'd attempted to dress down in order to better identify with his subordinates. Looking intently at her reflection in the mirror, she took in the form fitting cowl neck dark green dress that ended just above her knees. She'd paired the dress with a wide brown belt, thick dark brown tights and knee high, high heeled brown leather boots. Her lustrous brown hair had been braided and wrapped elaborately on the top of her head. Golden chandelier earrings glinted at her ears and a long gold chain hung down low from the decadent cowl on her dress. She looked like an exotic eastern princess.

Stan sauntered into the room attaching gold cufflinks to the cuffs of his cobalt blue shirt. Cecilia reluctantly admired the picture he presented with the deep blue of the shirt darkening his wintry blue eyes. He shrugged on a black suit coat over black dress pants. To finish off the ensemble, he wore a blue and grey striped tie. He stopped short to look her up and down. "Beautiful darling." He walked over to his dresser and pulled something out of the top drawer. "I have something for you to put in your purse."

Cecilia frowned as she grabbed her small designer handbag from the top of her dresser. "Here it is." She opened the leather purse and handed it to him.

Stan held up the object and showed it to her before dropping it into her handbag. "A little reminder to watch your tongue tonight." He handed the bag back to Cecilia who'd suddenly blush deep red. The object was a square shaped wooden hair brush. Up until this point, Stan hadn't used anything other than his bare hand to spank her. She thought that was painful enough. She couldn't imagine how painful the wooden hairbrush would be! Wincing apprehensively, Cecilia snapped the purse shut. She tried to ignore the sudden moisture in her nether regions.

*****

Stan escorted Cecilia into the large conference room at the bank that had been decorated lavishly for the office Christmas party. Cecilia looked around disdainfully at the bank employees enjoying their free booze and appetizers. Did Stan really expect her to cozy up to them all? "Let me take your coat and purse darling." Stan gallantly removed her fur edged leather coat after taking her handbag. "I'll put these items in my office so they'll be safe." He dropped a quick kiss to her cheek and turned away to walk out of the room to the hallway. Feeling slightly abandoned, Cecilia looked around at the party goers. She spotted Sarah on the edge of the room and gave a slight smile and a small wave to her. Sarah smiled brightly and waved back. Sarah's husband's muscular arm was wrapped firmly around her waist as if he couldn't stand to let her go. Cecilia looked on in envy as he nuzzled Sarah's cheek. They certainly were affectionate now. It didn't seem fair to Cecilia that she would have to wait five years to experience such closeness with Blaine. At this thought, she felt Stan's hard hand settle on her waist. She turned to smile at him and allowed him to steer her through the throng of people to the bar. "Would you like a drink sweetheart?" Stan leaned his head low to speak in her ear above the din of the crowd.

Cecilia nodded her head once sharply. "A glass of wine would be nice." She replied. Stan ordered for her and got a draft microbrew for himself. They sauntered around the room as Stan made sure to talk to as many of his employees as possible. Cecilia attempted to hide her boredom as he made small talk.

"Cecilia did you hear Brent's comment?"

Cecilia shook her head and smiled ruefully. "Sorry, I drifted away there for a second."

Stan's hand on the small of her back tightened. "Brent was just telling us about his new BMW."

Cecilia lifted her eyebrows and looked at the employee, uh Brent, in surprise. "How can you afford that?" She blurted out then lifted a hand to her mouth. Realizing her mistake, she attempted to backtrack. "Uh, I meant to say…congratulations." She smiled brightly at Brent while Stan's fingers now dug into her waist.

Stan made some polite conversation then stiffly led Cecilia away until they were in a corner. "I want you to go to my office and wait for me in the proper position on top of my desk." He whispered in her ear. "Place the brush on the desk next to you."

With pink cheeks, Cecilia kept her gaze on the ground as she nodded her understanding of his order. "Yes Sir." She scurried towards the exit.

Stan made the rounds for a few minutes after Cecilia exited the room then slowly made his way to the door. Making his escape, he quickly walked up the marble covered hallway to the mahogany door of his office. Looking around quickly, he opened the door and closed it. After locking the knob, he took in the sight that waited for him spread upon his desk. Cecilia had pulled up the skirt of her dark green sweater dress and pulled down the dark brown tights and her thong underwear to just above her knees revealing her pert ivory ass and thighs. She leaned over the top of his desk with hands splayed on the wood and her head turned to one side. The wooden hairbrush was placed right next to her head.

Stan waited for a moment by the door with his hands folded over his chest. "Cecilia, do you know what you did wrong?"

His wife nodded her head as it rested on the desk. "I spoke in a disrespectful fashion to one of your employees." Her voice shook as she spoke.

Stan briskly walked to the desk and picked up the hairbrush. "I'm going to give you ten with this. If you're good and don't try to cover up or get away, I'll allow you to climax tonight." He paused for a second. "Do you understand?"

Cecilia blinked back tears as she nodded her head. "Yes, Sir." As she shifted her hips nervously, Stan noted the sheen of moisture on her thighs and smiled triumphantly to himself. She was turned on by this turn of events. He lifted the brush and brought it down hard on her right buttock. Smack! Cecilia jumped at the impact. She looked frantically at her husband over her shoulder. "Stan, I'm not sure that I can..."

Sam stopped and crossed his arms. "Are you saying that you would like to divorce? That is your only choice. Either you submit to me or we go our separate ways. What do you want to do?"

With tears shimmering in her eyes, Cecilia nodded her head. "I'll submit to you."

He raised the brush again. Smack! Now her left buttock showed a bright red square. Cecilia subsided back down on the desk as two large tears started to run down her cheeks. Stan continued with her correction as she sobbed silently. Smack, smack, smack, smack, smack, smack, smack, smack! By the time he was done, her bare buttocks were bright red and slightly swollen. Stan smiled in satisfaction at the sight of her pussy juices dripping almost to her knees. He turned the brush around and delicately inserted just the tip of the handle into her swollen cunt lips. Cecilia's hips bucked up at the stimulation and she moaned as he penetrated her with the instrument of her torture. "Oh...Stan!" She groaned as he briskly fucked her with the brush. Her hips frantically worked her pussy on the wooden implement. Stan could tell that she was fast approaching her climax. He pulled out the brush and brusquely pulled up her underwear and tights and pulled down her sweater dress.

"Sorry, Love…you don't get to come until the evening is over." Cecilia moaned in denial. Stan helped her up to standing. He wiped her tears off of her cheeks with his thumb. "Please clean this off for me dear." He held the handle of the brush to her lipstick tinted lips. Cecilia's brown eyes narrowed at him for a moment before she delicately licked off the thick handle. "Take it all in please." Stan said in an implacable tone. Cecilia's eyes shot darts at him as she took the whole handle deep in her throat. Stan smiled in satisfaction as he removed the brush from her mouth. "Good girl." Cecilia internally rolled her eyes.

Stan took in her tear stained beauty before grabbing a tissue. "Let me wipe off your eyes so we can return to the party." He gently blotted her tears until they were all cleaned off. He hugged her close to his side before they returned to the group. Cecilia kept close to Stan's side as he introduced her to several of his employees. Though she couldn't be mistaken for being warm, Cecilia dealt with most of them in a satisfactory fashion. All of her good intentions went out the window when they talked to George and Brenda Johnson. George was one of her husband's VPs and they'd all socialized together a few times. Their last visit had been ruined by Cecilia suggesting to Brenda that she needed to lose some weight. Brenda seemed afraid to say anything to Cecilia and she kept her head lowered.

In an attempt to make conversation, Cecilia plucked at Brenda's sleeve. "So, did you try that buns and thighs DVD I suggested?" As the words left her lips, Cecilia knew that she'd crossed the line. Her hand flew up to cover her mouth. "Not that you need it. You look…great." The last comment came out of her mouth before she could stifle it. Stan's hand tightened on her elbow.

He leaned over to whisper in her ear. "Wait for me in the office." With her cheeks bright red and her head lowered, Cecilia dragged her feet all the way back to Stan's office.

Stan gently closed and locked the door as he entered the office. Cecilia was back in position with a now bright red posterior shining out between her upturned skirt and pulled down tights and underwear. The hairbrush sat ominously on the desk next to her.

Stan rolled up his sleeves and walk across the room to stand by her side. "Do you know what you did Cecilia?"

Cecilia nodded her head on the desk. The ornately braided hair on the top of her head managed to remain intact in this position. "Yes Sir. I was rude to Brenda. I…I shouldn't have mentioned the exercise DVD."

Stan picked up the hairbrush. "Exactly. In the future you will stay away from the subject of dieting or weight loss with my employees and their spouses. Do you understand?" He lightly tapped her ass with the brush as he spoke.

Cecilia nodded her head vigorously. "Yes Sir, I'll avoid speaking about weight loss and exercise with your employees in the future." A pause, then. "Do you really need to spank me again?" She shifted her hips uncomfortably with these words.

Stan ran a hand over her hot throbbing buttocks. "I want to reinforce this lesson Darling. I'll no longer ignore your nasty comments. Do you understand?"

Tears welled up in Cecilia's eyes again. "Yes I do. I…I promise that I will try harder."

Stan took a deep breath. "Okay, I'll make it quick and not too painful though you might have trouble sitting the next few days." He lifted the brush and brusquely administered her correction. Smack! Smack! Smack! Smack! Smack! Smack! Smack! Smack! Smack! Smack! By the time he was done, Cecilia had large tears running down her cheeks. After restoring her clothing, Stan pulled her up from the desk and lovingly wiped her face with his handkerchief. "I love you darling and I want the whole world to understand why I love you. Tempering your tongue will go a long way towards making them understand." He gathered her in his arms and pulled her against him.

Cecilia stiffly submitted to his embrace then melted and swayed against him. She locked her arms around his neck and pushed her pelvis up into his. "So, do you want to do something else on the top of your desk?" She asked with sultry eyes.

Stan regarded her steadily for a moment then dropped his head to place a hard kiss on her mouth. "Not yet Hon. Let's see how the rest of the evening goes." He wrapped an arm around her shoulders and escorted her back to the party.

*****

The rest of the party passed uneventfully. Stan and Cecilia made their way home after saying goodbye to the other partygoers. Once they were home, Cecilia stripped for Stan and willingly helped him to strip before dropping to her knees to suck at his penis. Once he was primed, she climbed up on the bed on all fours and presented her reddened backside to him in an obvious invitation to fuck. Shrugging ruefully, Stan took her up on her invitation and crawled up behind her and inserted his cock into her seeping vagina with one thrust. As he began to thrust heavily in her swollen slit, Cecilia started to rock back on his tool making sure that she got the deepest penetration. Stan reveled in the tight fit of her vagina as his hips pistoned against her chastened posterior. Stopping for a moment, Stan disengaged and attempted to turn Cecilia to her back. She fought him for a moment then reluctantly rolled over. Stan lovingly wrapped her legs around his back as he penetrated her clinging depths again. Wrapping the sides of her face with both of his hands, Stan attempted to maintain eye contact with his wife as he made love to her. Cecilia widened her eyes in alarm and then closed them while he started to increase the intensity of his thrusts. They both climaxed at the same time though Stan felt like they'd made no connection except at the point where their bodies joined.

After Cecilia's breathing deepened into the slow steady rhythm of sleep, Stan sat up on the side of the bed and ran his hands through the thick white blond hair covering his head. He stared at nothing for a moment before getting up to grab a robe and slippers. Walking down to his home office he opened his laptop and searched briefly on the web before finding the correct site. Clicking on an e-mail link, he typed in a succinct message and sent it. After sending the message and closing the laptop lid, he sat for a moment and looked at his faint reflection in the office window. Finally he shook his head as if to rid it of unwelcome thoughts and rose to go back to bed.

Chapter Three – Expert Advice

"Once the rules have been established and a domestic discipline routine has been enforced, your marital relationship should become increasingly emotionally intimate as well as physically intimate."
Excerpt from How to Be a Dominant Husband by Penelope Wiggins

The holidays passed by with little fanfare. On Christmas Eve, Stan presented Cecilia with a gorgeous diamond pendant necklace with matching solitaire diamond earrings. Cecilia gave him a handsome leather wallet. They both obligingly admired their gifts and ate the simple dinner Cecilia had prepared. On Christmas day they dutifully skyped their parents then spent the rest of the holiday lounging about the house. That evening Cecilia managed to instant message Blaine on Facebook while Stan watched a movie on TV.

"Hey Blaine, love, just wanted to wish you a Merry Christmas!" She typed with a slight smile.

Blaine's reply was almost instantaneous. "OMG. You are alive! Everything okay over there with Bluebeard?"

Cecilia smothered a laugh as she responded. "He's backed off a bit in the last few days. I'm hoping all will return to normal soon. All of this domesticity is really starting to get old!"

"LOL. I don't blame you. I have a difficult time seeing you all housewifey in an apron and shit."

Cecilia looked up at Stan quickly as she replied. "I actually have dishpan hands!"

"Say it isn't so!" Blaine answered.

Cecilia snorted. "I'd better sign off before Bluebeard gets suspicious. I love you!"

"Love you too Beautiful. Talk to you soon." Blaine closed down the chat window.

Closing her laptop with a sigh, Cecilia picked up her embroidery project and sat next to Stan on the couch without touching him.

Stan looked sideways at her. "Friends on Facebook good?"

Cecilia smiled at him brightly. "Just great. Sounds like their holidays went well." She looked at the embroidery pattern and started to fill in the area indicated with a bright blue thread. After looking at her steadily for a moment, Stan's attention turned back to the TV. They spent the rest of the evening in an uneasy silence.

*****

Stan was relieved to return to his office after the holiday break. He'd enforced their regular domestic discipline schedule over the holidays with daily maintenance spankings and weigh-ins. On the day after Christmas, Stan was pleased to see that Cecilia had gained five of the ten pounds he'd mandated. Cecilia, on the other hand, had spent the rest of the break attempting to sneak in extra exercise sessions. Stan shook his head at the thought of how sore her ass must be today. He'd paddled her at least once a day after that weigh-in for breaking his limited exercise rule.

Though she was mad at him for making her toe the line, Cecilia couldn't keep her hands off of him after a spanking. Stan smiled at the memories of Cecilia attempting to entice him to fuck her. She became a champion cocksucker, dropping to her knees in front of him where ever he was seated and unzipping his pants before engulfing his large penis in her mouth. He let her stroke him to a full erection many times and even came in her mouth at least once a day. Though she constantly enticed him, he'd only deigned to fuck her twice since Christmas. Both times she'd refused to look him in the eyes and seemed intent on using him just as a means to get an orgasm. Finally tiring of these unsatisfying encounters, Stan started to order her to use a dildo in front of him to satisfy her urges. She grudgingly accepted this poor substitute for his penis and fucked herself to orgasm at least once a day. Stan made her do it in the living room on the couch next to him and in their bed at night so he could watch. After she reached her climax, he ordered her to deep throat the dildo in order to clean it off. After she finished, Stan would often go to the bathroom and stroke himself off until he ejaculated. He knew that he really needed to come inside her in order to increase their chances of conceiving but he was having serious doubts about their relationship at this point.

Though domestic discipline had definitely enhanced their sex life but he didn't think that it had increased the emotional intimacy of their marriage at all. Unless she was horny, Cecilia didn't want to touch him and in fact, even shied away from cuddling with him in the evening. He sighed and shook his head in resignation. Maybe he should just let her go with a large settlement and call it good. He dropped his head into his hands. Unfortunately, he actually loved the shrew. He was certain that the sweet yielding young woman he'd fallen in love with five years ago was somewhere under Cecilia's hard exterior. The cell phone rang on the top of his desk, interrupting his thoughts. Stan frowned at the unknown number and answered. "Stan Bergstrom here. How can I help you?"

There was a small pause then a clear English voice carried through the phone. "Mr. Bergstrom, pardon me for taking so long to get back to you. This is Penelope Wiggins…the author of How to Be a Dominant Husband."

Stan looked down at the phone in amazement. "Mrs. Wiggins. Thank you for calling. I just assumed that you'd e-mail me back." His voice trailed off.

He could hear a smile in her voice as she answered. "After reading your e-mail I decided that your case merited a phone consultation."

Stan tried to keep the emotion out of his voice. "Thank you…I'm just not sure where to go from here. Cecilia actually seems to thrive sexually under threat of spanking but I…I don't think that our emotional attachment is any better than before. She doesn't seem to want my touch and refuses to cuddle with me." His voice broke. "I'm afraid that I've lost her and I don't know what to do."

Mrs. Wiggin's brisk voice broke in. "From your e-mail I understand that you basically coerced your wife into this arrangement?"

Stan nodded his head shamefacedly then realized that she couldn't see him. "Uh, yes. I didn't know what else to do. She was out of control…bitchy, indulging in excessive shopping, starving herself to the point of starvation. I was really concerned about her." He stopped to swallow nervously. "She wasn't like this when I met her. I don't know what happened."

"Hmmm…I can understand your concern Stan. Unfortunately, it is possible that it may be too late to save your marriage." Mrs. Wiggins stopped as if deep in thought. Then she resumed. "So tell me, how would you describe your wife's relationship with her parents?"

Stan laughed bitterly. "Her dad is okay but her mom is a bitchy nightmare."

"Do you think that her mother spent much time with Cecilia as a baby and child?"

Stan snorted. "Not likely. She had a fleet of nannies and refused to breastfeed because it would ruin her figure. In fact, Cecilia is an only child because her mother couldn't tolerate the thought of another pregnancy."

Mrs. Wiggins prompted. "So when you two first met?"

Stan continued. "Cecilia was softer…nicer. I just don't know what happened."

"Okay, so she'd gotten progressively thinner and more brittle as the years have passed. Can you make any guesses as to why this personality change has occurred?" Mrs. Wiggins inquired.

Stan's lips firmed into a thin line. "I think the group of rich bitches she runs with might partially be at fault. I noticed her attitude changing soon after she began hanging out with them."

"Ahhh…okay. So I'm thinking that there might be a combination of factors at work here. I think that Cecilia probably didn't bond with her mother as a child. When she met you, she was flooded with the hormones related to falling in love so you saw a softer, gentler Cecilia. She also probably had a better level of sex hormones at that time because she had more body fat and a regular period. A painfully thin woman's body can't produce sex hormones which is why they don't have periods. Progesterone is the 'get along' hormone so if a woman has low levels of this hormone, you'll see more bitchy behavior." She took a deep breath. "You are already addressing the weight problem. I think what you should do now is concentrate on bonding with your wife. Usually, regular orgasms will release oxytocin, the bonding hormone, but that doesn't seem to be enough in her case. It makes me wonder if her affections are directed elsewhere…" She seemed to collect herself then continued. "So what I suggest is that you should get her on a regular schedule of nipple stimulation."

Stan broke in incredulously. "Nipple stimulation?"

She laughed. "Yes. Nipple stimulation will increase the production of oxytocin which should foster a bonded relationship between the two of you. In your e-mail you happened to mention that the two of you have been trying to conceive for years. Is that correct?"

Stan nodded as he answered. "Yes for the last three years."

"Have you looked into adoption?"

Stan frowned, wondering what tack the conversation was taking. "Uh, yeah we are on the lists at a few different agencies just as a back up."

"So, it is possible that you may adopt if you don't conceive in the next year?"

Stan pursed his lips. "Yess…"

Mrs. Wiggins jumped in. "So, what I am thinking is that you suggest regular nipple stimulation as a means to facilitate breastfeeding in case you end up adopting a child."

Stan frowned. "And by nipple stimulation you mean…?"

She laughed. "Sucking on them my dear." She continued. "If you were just attempting to induce lactation, I'd suggest you rent a breast pump and set up a regular pumping schedule. She'd need to do it at regular intervals at least eight times a day to induce lactation." She paused. "In your case the focus is bonding and intimacy, not lactation so she will need you to stimulate her breasts instead of a machine. I would suggest you attempt to have at least four to five sessions a day. You will need to work up to at least ten minutes per breast in each session."

Stan was dumbfounded. "Okay…Do you think that will really work?"

"Oh yes dear. I've seen it help many couples who want to increase the emotional intimacy in their relationship." She cleared her throat. "One caveat in your case. Your wife should show some signs of bonding within two weeks of starting this stimulation routine. If she still seems distant emotionally at the end of this time period I am afraid that it may be too late. You will need to prepare yourself for this eventuality."

Stan swallowed nervously. "Okay."

Mrs. Wiggins cut in. "Also dear, I need to warn you that this type of relationship is a major commitment on the part of the husband. There will come a time when your wife will be both emotionally and physically dependent on your attentions. Though it is doubtful that she will produce milk, it is likely that her breasts will swell when a session is due and will become increasingly uncomfortable if a session is missed. You will need to be present to give her ease if such an eventuality occurs." She took a deep breath. "So, if either of you need to travel, you will need to do it together or she will be incredibly uncomfortable. Do you understand?" This in a stern tone.

Stan sat up straight as if she could see him. "Yes Ma'am."

Mrs. Wiggins released a trill of laughter. "Okay Stan. I'll give you some pointers as far as specifics. Please check in with me at two weeks into this regimen let me know how things are going. Okay?"

Stan readily replied. "Okay." Mrs. Wiggins made a sound of assent and began to instruct Stan on the intricacies of nipple stimulation.

*****

That evening Stan and Cecilia sat and ate their home prepared meal in almost absolute silence. Stan asked Cecilia how things went at the Daycare and she shrugged her shoulders and grunted as if nothing of consequence occurred. After making a few more conversational gambits, Stan finally gave up and finished his dinner in silence. He sat and watched Cecilia sulkily eat the portions of food he'd dished up for her. After she was done, he helped her clear the table and turned to grab her arm as she headed out of the kitchen to the living room. "We need to talk for a moment before you pull out your laptop." He led her to the living room and indicated that she sit on a chair.

She sat back with arms folded over her chest, a mutinous just to her chin. "What now?"

Stan sat in the chair opposite hers leaned forward with his elbows on his thighs then laced his fingers together. "So, when was the last time you had your period."

Cecilia sat forward in outrage. "What business is that of yours?"

Stan gave her a steady look and replied. "I'm your husband and we are trying to get pregnant." He continued. "You can't get pregnant if you aren't having your period."

Cecilia sat back and stuck out her lower lip. "I don't know, maybe four months ago."

Stan looked at her intently with steely blue eyes. "So, it is possible that you just aren't going to be able to get pregnant."

Cecilia shrugged. "Possibly." Her attitude was unconcerned.

Stan continued. "Remember how we talked about adopting?"

Cecilia's eyes opened in alarm. "Yes?"

"And how we applied to a few agencies…?"

"Yes." Cecilia answered guardedly.

Stan smiled at her in excitement. "It looks like we might be able to get a child placed with us in the next year!"

Cecilia's eyes opened wide in horror. She really didn't want a brat. She'd just gone along with Stan in his quest for an heir. She frantically searched her brain for a possible gambit but couldn't think of anything that would keep her married to Stan for the needed period of time. She stilled for a second. A baby meant child support! Maybe this wasn't such a bad idea. She dropped her folded arms and smiled at Stan in a faux excited fashion. "That is fantastic news!" How soon will we be able to get a placement?"

Stan coughed into his hand and continued. "Probably sometime in the next year. So I think we should start preparing you for the baby's arrival."

Cecilia's eyes narrowed. "Prepare me…what do you mean?"

Stan smiled at her in a smug fashion. "Why to breastfeed of course."

Cecilia fell back against the chair in shock. "What!" She screeched. "I don't plan to breast feed."

Stan shook his head in a sadly. "So I guess I should start the divorce proceedings. I consider this preparation another form of submission to my will. If you aren't ready to breastfeed my children, I don't want to have children with you.

Cecilia stared at him in horror with huge brown eyes. She could tell that he was serious….crap! She wrapped her arms around her slender waist. "So what does this stimulation entail?"

Stan rubbed his hands together. "We will need to do at least four to five sessions a day where I suck on each breast about ten minutes."

The words came out slowly. "You'll do it? I thought that most people use machines..."

Stan's eyes darkened. "As your dominant I've decided that I will do all of the stimulation. As you know, your body is mine to do with as I wish...right?"

At his prompting Cecilia blinked rapidly and nodded her head. "Uh, right." Her tone reflected disgust with this turn of events.

Stan slapped his hands together startling Cecilia. "Okay, well there's no time like to present to get started." He stood up and walked over to stand by the couch. "We'll be doing about four to five sessions a day at regular intervals. First session will be early in the morning when we wake up. Second session will be at lunch. Third session will be when I come home from work in the evening before dinner. Fourth session will be at bedtime and I plan to wake up in the middle of the night for the final session."

He held up a hand with the fingers folded. "The rules for you concerning nipple stimulation are. One.." He held up one finger. "You wear bras and clothing that give me easy access. I want you to sleep naked to aid in this matter." He held up another finger. "Two, you will be open to me during these sessions. Either you will straddle my crotch or you will open your legs for me so I can have easy access while I'm stimulating your nipples. No underwear is allowed and I want you to cut out the crotch of all of your tights. I don't want any barriers between us." He held up a third finger. "Finally, if I request you to expose either your breasts or your pussy for me, you will immediately comply or face punishment." He paused. "Do you understand?" Looking at him with huge eyes, Cecilia nodded slowly.

Stan sat down on the couch and motioned for her to get up and stand next to him. "Remove your underwear and straddle my crotch." Cecilia complied with shaking hands, dropping her thong onto the coffee table by the couch. As she lowered herself onto his fabric covered crotch, Cecilia noted that his erection was already stirring to life. "Unbutton your top and take off your bra." Cecilia had so much difficulty in undoing the clasp on her bra; Stan finally released it for her. Small pink tipped nipples bounced on her pert size B breasts as they fell out of the lace edged wisp of a bra. Stan stopped for a moment to admire her beauty. Her breasts stood out proudly from her bony ribcage. They were surprisingly big considering her otherwise emaciated frame.

Stan lifted one breast then the other in his large hand. A calloused thumb rubbed over the pink tip of her left breast. Looking up at Cecilia, Stan leaned forward and engulfed about half of the breast in his mouth. Her nipple ended up pressed against the roof by his tongue. Once he got her in position, Stan started gently suckling on the breast in an oddly light rapid fashion. Almost immediately, Cecilia felt a pinching sensation in her womb and then a zing to her clitoris. Oddly enough after about two minutes of stimulation, she also felt thirsty. Stan let go of her breast and looked up at her. "Place your hands on my shoulders." Cecilia hesitantly complied as he turned his attention back to the now distended wet nipple. She held herself stiffly as he continued. After what had to be at least five minutes, Stan gently released her left breast and turned his attention to her right one. As he continued his ministrations, Cecilia found herself relaxing and softening against him. Her hips started to gently rock against the rock hard erection pressing against her clit. She also had to stop herself from stroking his hair. Mmmm...a nap sounded really good right now. As she slumped against him, Stan finished up on the right breast and gently disengaged. He wrapped his arms around his wife's waist and gently held her in his embrace.

Cecilia finally leaned back and sleepily blinked her eyes. "I should really check my e-mails and Facebook now before I fall asleep." Stan smiled at her obvious attempts to keep her eyes open. He deftly latched her bra into place and buttoned her dress. Grabbing her by the waist, he lifted her off of his erection.

"Better go do that Hon." He said quietly while smoothing her hair. Cecilia blinked slowly again then seemed to wake up.

"Okay." She languidly stood up and sat in the chair next to her laptop. Yawning hugely, she opened up the computer and rapidly checked her e-mails and Facebook. No messages from Blaine. Darn! Stifling a yawn she walked back to the couch and started working on her embroidery. Next thing she knew, she was being carried in Stan's strong arms. His distinctive fresh air scent seemed stronger than usual. Without thinking, Cecilia buried her nose into his chest and inhaled his masculine fragrance. She heard a chuckle under her ear.

"I'll get you into bed in just a moment Sweetheart." She could feel Stan's arm move to pull back the covers of the bed. He sat her on the edge and quickly stripped off her clothing. He laid her back against her pillow and pulled the covers up to her chin. "I'll be in to bed in just a minute Hon." She heard his footfalls as he walked to the bathroom. Later she drowsily felt him climb into bed. He rolled over to press against her side. "Time for the next session Cecee." She barely had time to express irritation at the annoying nickname before she felt Stan's head dip under the covers to capture her breast. Before he started, he took a hand and pushed her legs apart so her pussy was exposed. The other hand captured her breast and his mouth took the now familiar position with the nipple pressed against the roof of his mouth. As he suckled, his free hand slid down over her bare pudendum and gently began to press rhythmically on the mons right above her clit. Cecilia's hips rocked in time to his gentle stimulation. She could feel herself slowly ramping up towards an orgasm. She attempted to hurry it along by thrusting her hips up into Stan's hand. She almost screamed in frustration as Stan pulled the hand away. He disengaged from her breast and came out from under the covers. "All in good time darling. Now roll onto your side and offer the other breast to me with your hand." Cecilia shifted as instructed. Stan dove back down under the covers and insinuated a hard thigh between her legs against her swollen, needy clit. Cecilia moaned low in her throat as he attended to the other breast. She subtly rocked her mons against his thigh as he diligently went to work. When he finished stimulating the breast, he came out from under the covers and cupped Cecilia's face with palms on either side. Looking deeply into her eyes, he dropped a hard kiss on her mouth as his thigh pressed hard against her sensitized clit. Cecilia felt herself tip over the edge into one of the hardest orgasms she'd ever experienced. Stan stayed right with her, his arms wrapped around her in a tight embrace. As she came out of it, the first thing she heard was Stan whispering in her ear. The second thing she felt was his arms holding her close. She buried her head in his chest and inhaled his fresh air scent before falling fast asleep.

Sometime in the middle of the night, Stan woke her up enough to position her correctly then set to work on her right breast. Cecilia drowsily cupped the back of his head with one hand before falling back to sleep. She woke up briefly when he moved her on her side so he could access the left breast. She had to hold the breast up for him in this position until he was placed correctly then she fell back into a sound slumber. She didn't remember anything else until she was woken by Stan again early the next morning. By this time her nipples were incredibly sensitive and she winced as Stan began to stimulate her right breast. Oddly enough, her pussy started weeping almost immediately. She could feel Stan smile against her body when he discovered the moisture with his free hand. He stuck two fingers in her cunt and kept them there during the whole session. Cecilia woke up completely after he finished her second breast and removed his fingers from her clinging channel without giving her release. She mutely pushed her pubis up against his hand. Then she buried her face in his neck and whispered. "Please...if nothing else can I use the dildo?"

Stan gave her an appraising look before answering. "I think all of your orgasms are going to be mine from now on. Right now, I don't choose to give you one. If you are a good girl today and submit to me sweetly today, I promise that you will get to come." He tapped her on the nose. "Now it's time for your maintenance spanking and weigh-in my dear. Time to get up!"

Cecilia groaned and sat up in bed. She looked down at her body, remembering suddenly that she'd slept nude. She blushed at the sight of her normally small light pink nipples now dark red and poking out at least a half an inch from the areola. Cupping her breasts in both hands, she lifted them up further to examine the beard rash Stan had left on them during their last session. She looked up at Stan with big eyes. "They're so sore. I don't know if I can do this four to five times a day."

He smiled and reached into his bedside table. "I bought this for you. I figured you might need it. You'll need to apply it after every stimulation session. If you want, I can do it for you." With these words, he opened the top on the small jar of cream and gently smoothed it over her tender crests. Cecilia felt almost immediate relief from the pain.

"Oh...thank you!" The words broke out from her lips.

Stan stopped and looked at her curiously for a moment then responded. "I'm your husband. It's my job to take care of you." He capped the jar and handed it to Cecilia. "You should carry this just in case you need it during the day." His eyes darkened to navy blue. "I don't know if I'll be able to restrict myself to four or five times a day so you might need to apply it frequently." Cecilia blushed and dropped her head.

Stan patted his thighs expectantly. "Let's get that maintenance spanking over with so we can get on with our day."

Cecilia slid over his lap into the proper position. She'd been spanked enough in the last few weeks, she knew what to expect. Placing her hands on the floor, she spread her legs open wide while Stan rubbed his hand proprietarily over her ass. She could feel some faint soreness left over from all of the spankings she'd received during the holiday break. Without warning, Stan gave a few warm up slaps to her buttocks and thighs then increased the intensity of his spanks until Cecilia had to blink rapidly to hold back her tears. As if sensing she were on the brink. Stan stopped the spanking and rubbed her buttocks to ease the pain. "Time for weigh-in." He led her to the bathroom and waited for her while she peed. After wiping and flushing the toilet, Cecilia walked over to the scale and stepped on. "You've gained a total of six pounds darling. That's excellent! Only four more to go." He tallied her weight on the chart and walked over to the bathroom door. "I think that all you need to wear today while making breakfast is this robe and a pair of slippers." Cecilia's cheeks warmed up as she slipped on the sheer, thigh length robe. Her reddened nipples stood out obscenely through the transparent fabric. The slippers he'd chosen were the frilly and slightly high heeled. As she walked into the kitchen, Cecilia felt like a pin up girl from the fifties. Knowing now what Stan wanted for breakfast, she automatically set to making his favorite breakfast of an omelet and toast. She also made a one egg omelet for herself hoping that would be enough to appease Stan.

Fresh from his shower, Stan walked into the kitchen while adjusting his cufflinks. "What a wonderful sight to greet me in the morning." He dropped a kiss on the top of her head. "What's for breakfast?" He inquired as he took a seat at the breakfast bar.

Cecilia tottered over to him in her transparent frilly robe and high heels holding a plate of food. "I made you an omelet and toast." She set it in front of him.

Stan smiled at her approvingly. "Looks fantastic, Love. You've really done well in your cooking lessons." He picked up his fork and started eating. She brought over her plate and Stan stopped to look at it. "One egg?" Cecilia nodded. "Did you include any meat or cheese?" Cecilia shook her head no. "Okay, I want to see you have either some toast or a piece of fruit with this." Cecilia glared at him and grabbed a banana out of the bowl on the counter. Stan shook his finger at her. "Watch your temper my dear. I'd hate to have to withhold your orgasm today." With these words he smiled down at his plate and took another bite. Cecilia fumed as she sat down with her food. Submitting to his food rules had been one of the biggest challenges for her in the last few weeks. Her anxiety about being overweight ramped up every time Stan weighed her and she'd gained some weight. She sighed and picked at her plate. Knowing that Stan would sit there all morning to make sure she finished it, she slowly ate every bit. Stan also finished his breakfast and threw back the last bit of coffee in his cup. "It's almost time for me to go." He handed his plate and cup to his wife who placed them on the counter on top of the dishwasher. "Cecelia, come over here before I leave." She gave him a narrow eyed gaze before complying with his order. Stan untied her sheer robe and exposed her bright red nipples to the harsh morning light. Smoothing the fabric to the side, Stan took in the beauty laid out before him. From his seat on the barstool height stool, he leaned forward and gently drew one ruby tipped breast into his mouth and suckled it into a diamond hard point. Sitting back he looked in satisfaction at his handiwork before leaning over to treat its mate to the same attention. After disengaging he kissed each breast in turn before standing up to look his wife in the eyes and dropping a hard kiss on her cheek. "Mine." He stated and then strode out of the kitchen to the mudroom. Cecilia heard him grab his coat before exiting into the garage. She hurried to clean up the breakfast mess then ran to get ready for her cooking class.

*****

Cecilia hurried down the hallway of the bank. Stan had decided that he wanted her to bring him lunch in the office today. After she attended her cooking class that morning, she'd quickly whipped up a simple homemade soup and two sandwiches for her husband and herself. Knowing that Stan was a stickler for punctuality, she wanted to be at his office as close to noon as possible. Remembering to smile at Stan's secretary as she passed, she knocked lightly on his door. "Come in." His voice rumbled with authority.

    Cecilia peered around the edge of the door and raised her eyebrows. "I've brought you some lunch."

    He smiled at her. His wintry blue eyes darkened in approval at her appearance. She'd worn a designer wrap dress in order to be more accessible for him. She'd paired it with tights and high heeled boots. Over the whole lot, she'd worn her usual fur trimmed leather coat. Stan motioned her to come into the office. "Lock the door." He told her in a low voice. Standing up, he walked to her side and took the bag containing their lunch out of her hand. Setting the bag on his desk, he grabbed her shoulders and twirled her around. He deftly removed the coat from her shoulders and threw it over a chair in the corner. "I think I want to sip on your beauties before we eat our lunch." Blushing up at him, Cecilia loosened the tie at the waist of her dress and revealed her lacy bra. Unlatching the front closure clasp, she exposed her breasts for his view. She'd obviously recently applied the ointment to them. They glistened from it. Stan ran a rough thumb over one nipple than the other. "Are you pretty sore?" He inquired.

    Cecilia nodded her head. "It was especially sensitive in the shower."

    Stan nodded his head in satisfaction. "Between your sore cheeks and your sore nipples I think you have sufficient reminders of who you belong to." He reached up to rub her cheek with his thumb. "Don't you think Darling?" Cecilia nodded her head reluctantly. She was finding that her thoughts focused more and more on pleasing Stan every day. Stan's hands gripped her waist and drew her towards the loveseat on the side of his office. "Straddle me while I stimulate your breasts." Cecilia immediately knelt over him with her skirt hiked up. Stan stopped for a moment. "Pull up the front of your skirt CeCee." Frowning at his use of her dreaded nickname, Cecilia lifted up the skirt to expose her denuded crotch peeking out from the opening in her tights. "Nice..." He drawled then settled her soppy lips right over the bulge in his dress pants. Realizing that she might leave a huge wet spot, Stan decided to unbutton and then unzip his dress pants revealing a semi-erect penis peeking out from behind the opened zipper. Cecilia groaned as she was settled over his burgeoning erection. Stan began energetically sucking on her left breast while running his hands over her torso. Cecilia started to involuntarily rock over his cock with small groans emanating from the back of her throat. Stan released her breast then whispered in her ear. "Lift up on your knees, Love." Frowning at him in puzzlement, Cecilia pushed herself up using his shoulders. When she felt the blunt tip of his erection teasing her swollen labia, Cecilia offered up a silent Glory Hallelujah. Stan grasped her waist with his hands and pulled her down roughly on his giant cock. Cecilia gasped at the depth of penetration in this position. Her internal muscles started rippling over the length of his large invader. "No moving up and down." He whispered. "Only penetration. Let's see if you can come from that alone." He returned to her left breast. Cecilia felt her silken sheath clench and release on his member as he continued with his ministrations. Stan was pleased to note that his wife's breathy moans and sobbing breaths increased as he switched to the other breast. The contractions around his cock continued to increase in frequency until Cecilia arched back and her vagina clamped down on his member. She started shaking as copious fluids released around his penis. After she reached her climax, she collapsed breathing heavily with her head on his shoulder. Stan released her breast and turned his head to catch her lips in a passionate kiss. She returned the kiss with fervor almost clicking teeth with him. She was still shaking with the intensity of her orgasm. Stan withdrew his cock from her vagina with another rush of fluid. He caught it with his handkerchief and wiped her off as best he could. He draped his wife across his lap and held her in his arms. He gently rocked her as she returned to normal. Once her breathing patterns normalized, Stan tilted her head up so her melting brown eyes could meet his. "Time for lunch." He grabbed the insulated lunch bag and unloaded the sandwiches. Unwrapping one, he hand Cecilia half of the sandwich. "Eat up." Drowning in his eyes, Cecilia held his gaze while biting into the sandwich. They ate in silence with eyes locked.

Chapter Five – Submission

"When your wife makes the decision to fully submit to you, you will feel like the luckiest man on earth." **Excerpt from How to Be a Dominant Husband by Penelope Wiggins**

Cecilia pushed back from the office desk at Tiny Sprouts with a sigh. After volunteering at the non-profit for the last few months, she'd managed to get all of their books in order and the office organized. With a sigh, she looked around the office suddenly at loose ends. She leaned back in the chair and crossed her arms over her chest. The sensitivity she felt in her nipples from the pressure of her arms over them led to a sudden clenching in her vagina. She looked at the clock. Almost time to go home. She couldn't wait to see Stan. She'd started to notice a full sensation in her breasts when a stimulation session was due. Only Stan's suckling seemed to remove the discomfort. Stan…she smiled to herself thinking of him. For some reason, she'd started to miss him during the day when they were separated. She was happy to see him come home every night and had started to cuddle close to him on the couch after dinner. During their nipple stimulation sessions she often ended up caressing his head and smiling down at him fondly. She was afraid to admit it to herself but it felt like she was falling back in love with her husband!

As her feelings deepened, her need to submit to him had also increased. Cecilia found herself following his rules without much thought on her part. She'd gained the required ten pounds plus a little bit more. Rather than worrying about whether she would get fat or worrying about whether her friends would look down on her, she was happy that she'd pleased her husband. Stan's fascination with her new sleek curves also helped her get over her misgivings. Sighing happily, Cecilia pushed back from the desk and grabbed her purse. Retrieving her coat from the back of her chair, she pulled it on as she walked through the daycare. "Goodbye Stacy!" Smiling from the corner where she helped a toddler into his coat and boots,

Stacy waved goodbye. Cecilia climbed into her car and started the ignition. As she drove the car out of the parking lot, her throbbing breasts reminded her that soon she'd be home to Stan and relief.

*****

Stan wheeled his Jaguar around a corner as he drove home from work. A giddy feeling rose in his chest the closer he got to home. He couldn't wait to get to Cecilia. Over the last three weeks he'd seen a major change in his shrewish wife. Cecilia now seemed happy to see him when he came home. Their regular nipple stimulation sessions had become the linchpins of their relationship. He smiled as he drove into their garage. Jumping eagerly out of the car he strode through the garage to the door into the mudroom and opened it impatiently. Hanging up his coat on a hook in the mudroom, he entered the kitchen to find his wife making the final touches to a roast in the oven. Seeing him enter, she covered the meat with a lid and turned the oven down to a slow cook setting. Smoothing an apron over her lap, she matter of factly started to unbutton her dress and unlatch one of the cups on her bra. Stan grabbed her hand as he walked through the kitchen to the living room. "God, I need you today." He muttered as he sat on the couch. As per their usual routine, Cecilia settled herself over his lap then lifted up as he unzipped his pants. His monster cock sprang up from the opened zipper and Cecilia lowered her well lubricated vagina over his erect member. They both groaned as Stan's cock bottomed out deep in Cecilia's abdomen. Stan grabbed his wife's narrow waist and pushed her back from him a bit. Running his eyes up and down her sleek form, he smiled at the changes he saw. The extra weight she'd gained had settled in her breasts, hips and thighs leaving her with a lovely curvaceous figure. His fingers tightened on her tiny waist as he moved her so her breast would be in the correct position for his attentions. He lifted one hand to heft the lovely orb in one palm and examined the changes he'd wrought. Over the course of the last few months, her petite pink tipped B cup breasts had grown to a heavy D cup with large dark brown areolas and inch long brown nipples. Stan ran a thumb lightly over the tracery of blue veins that had recently appeared over the sides. They might need to back off on the number of sessions. He mused to himself. It looked like her breasts were on the verge of producing milk. He could cut out the night time session…though he enjoyed Cecilia's sleepy submission to his demands. Hmmm….he'd have to think on it further. Dismissing these thoughts from his head, he leaned forward and took the engorged breast into his mouth. Cecilia sighed in relief as he started sucking. She'd become more and more dependent on these sessions to relief her discomfort. They both had noticed a softening in the breast tissue when he was done.

When he was almost done with the breast, Stan felt soft hands gliding through his hair then a soft kiss to the top of his head. "Hard day at work Dear?" A soft pulsing occurred in the warm tissue surrounding his cock.

He gently released the now wet distended nipple. "I had to fire a teller today for stealing." He sighed. "She will be going to jail I am sure. I'm worried about her children. She was their sole means of support."

Cecilia continued to caress his head. "Should I look into it and find out if they have family to take care of them?" She rocked gently on the huge invader inside her.

Stan looked up into her eyes in appreciation. "That would be wonderful Darling." He hugged her close for a moment, then leaned back. "I'm ready for the other side."

Looking into his navy blue eyes with deep chocolate pools, Cecilia deftly fastened the cup on the breast he'd just suckled and released the cup on the other side. Holding the heavy orb up in her hand, Cecilia leaned forward to offer it to her husband. Stan's lips engulfed the front half and he set to work. Cecilia's hands returned to caress his heads and shoulders. The fluttering around his cock intensified as he attended to the second breast. Breaking free for a moment, he looked up into his wife's burning eyes. "Don't come until I give you permission."

Cecilia nodded her head. "Yes Sir." He saw acceptance of his mastery over her body in her eyes. Feeling incredibly blessed, he returned to the breast. Once he'd sufficiently stimulated the nipple, he released it from his mouth.

"I want to see both of them while I fuck you." Cecelia smiled complacently as she unlatched the other cup. The covered breast spilled out from the opening in the bra. Both orbs hung down slightly lower than they had before he'd nursed on them. He admired the way the long nipples drooped a little, pointing down. He grabbed her narrow waist tightly with both hands. "Put your hands on my shoulder." Cecilia complied. Stan started working her up and down on his rock hard penis. Cecilia compliantly allowed his use of her body while letting out small gasps and moans. The rippling around his cock increased and tightened as he slammed her clit down on his pelvis. Her heavy breasts jiggled up and down looking oddly incongruous peeking out from the openings in the nursing bra. To the accompaniment of her disappointed groan, Stan lifted her off of his member and turned to lay her down on the couch. "You can come anytime you want now. Okay Love?" He sunk into her cunt balls deep with these words while draping her legs over his shoulders. Cecilia nodded frantically. Strands of mink brown hair stuck to the sweat on her cheeks. Stan grabbed her wrists and held them over her head as he began to shaft her hard and fast. Her full breasts bounced up and down with each thrust, almost grazing her chin on the upswing. Looking up into Stan's eyes helplessly, Cecilia arched into a massive orgasm. Her silken sheath clamped down on Stan's penis almost painfully. Stan shouted and let loose a huge stream of cum into her receptive body. Cecilia's muscular passage started to milk it up towards her womb. Stan held himself deep in her body until the muscular contractions around his cock eased. Releasing her hands, he gently slid her legs off of his shoulders and leaned forward to cup her cheeks in his palms. Looking into her slumberous brown eyes he kissed her gently on full pink lips. "Thank you Cecee. That went a long way towards making my day better." Cecilia's cheeks tinted pink at his compliment. Her cunt clenched tightly one more time around his penis then Stan withdrew. He caught the stream of their bodily fluids with his handkerchief as he kneeled up on the couch. Looking down at his ravaged wife, Stan had a satisfied smile on his face as he matter of factly wiped off his penis and zipped it back into his pants. Leaning forward, he wiped his wife's crotch off in much the same fashion. Her swollen red clit peeked at out him from between her hairless outer lips as he tended to her. Flipping the skirt of her dress down, he offered Cecilia a hand. Smiling at him tremulously, she accepted his help up. Her still uncovered breasts bobbled as she came to standing. "Don't cover them up. I want to look at them during dinner." With blazing red cheeks, Cecelia nodded her assent and scurried back to the kitchen. She needed to get dinner on the table.

Cecilia waited until Stan had seated himself at the dining table before she served him his dinner. She took in his fresh air scent as she leaned over his right shoulder to set down his plate of food. To her mortification, her enlarged breasts now hung down far enough for her nipples to brush his shoulder as she withdrew. For his part, Stan's eyes darkened in appreciation at the sight of her unfettered beauties dangling next to his head. He complimented himself on his idea of taking her to a maternity store last weekend to buy nursing bras. Her breasts had outgrown all of her old bras and Stan wanted easy access to them at any time. Nursing bras seemed like the perfect solution to him. After all, she would need them when she fed their child! With this logic, he'd talked her into buying several sturdy black lace bras with detachable cups.

Cecilia strode back towards the kitchen then stopped for a moment and turned with her hands clasped together. "Can I get you anything else...any other beverage than water?"

Stan smiled at her warmly. "No Dear. Serve yourself a plate and sit down. I want to eat with my gorgeous wife." Her cheeks blushed at his compliment as she turned to get her plate from the kitchen. After she seated herself and began to eat, Stan paused in taking a bite from his fork to ask. "So, how was your day?"

Cecilia looked at him with a slight smile. "It went well. I finally got the office organized at the daycare. I'm going to need to start helping with the children now if I want to keep myself busy." She frowned down at her long nails. "I'm going to have to get these removed if I want to work with the babies. Stacy told me that fake nails can sometimes harbor a fungus that is dangerous for little ones." She shrugged dismissively. "To tell you the truth, they are getting in the way when I cook and do embroidery. I don't think I'll miss them." Stan's eyebrows raised high in amazement but he didn't comment.

"Uh, Stan?" Cecilia's voice sounded hesitant.

"Yes dear?" He looked up at her mildly.

She tangled her fingers together. "One of my friends called to see if I could meet them for lunch this week." She leaned forward eagerly. "I haven't seen any of them since you...since we..." She faltered.

"Since you submitted to me?" Stan offered.

Pink tinged her cheeks again. "Yes. I understand why you didn't want me to see them while I was gaining weight but now that I've gained it…"

Stan laid his fork down by his plate looked at her steadily. "Do you think you will feel comfortable around them now that you are larger?"

She looked down at her hands. "I think so."

Stan sighed heavily then returned to his food. "Okay, I'll allow you to go on Thursday afternoon." He paused for a moment. "You should come to my office beforehand so you aren't uncomfortable during the luncheon."

At this reminder of their interdependent relationship, Cecilia's cheeks blazed red. She picked up her fork and speared a piece of broccoli. "I will." She promised.

*****

Later that evening Cecilia checked her e-mails and Facebook. Her bare breasts still spilled out of the front of her unbuttoned bodice. As bedtime approached they'd started to firm up and weren't hanging quite so low. She was already anticipating the relief she'd gain in just an hour. She clicked on the Message icon on the left side of screen. Several messages were from Blaine. Her brow wrinkled slightly as she read his posts. "Are you okay? I haven't heard from you for days." The next message read. "I'm worried about you. Has your husband forbidden you from talking to me?" She scrolled down to the last one. "If I don't hear from you soon, I'm calling the police." At his dramatic declaration, she shook her head. Talking with Blaine just didn't seem as important to her anymore. Her newfound feelings for Stan dominated all aspects of her life. Unfortunately, she'd neglected to respond to Blaine's messages in the last few weeks because she'd wanted to cuddle with her husband.

Smiling grimly, she attempted to perform damage control. "Hey buddy. Sorry I haven't been on FB much lately. Call off the authorities. I'm fine." She stopped for a moment to think. "I'm much busier now and just don't have the time to check FB more than a few times a week. Sorry about that!" She added a smiley face.

She hoped her response would mollify him. She shook her head at the memory of how infatuated she'd been with him for the last few years. On some level, she'd always known that Blaine was a boy in comparison to her manly husband. If she'd actually left Stan for Blaine, she knew that she would have eventually regretted it. Sighing heavily, she closed the laptop and set it on the side table. She stood up and walked over to her husband on the couch. Grabbing a chenille throw, she curled up next to Stan. Engrossed in his program, Stan absently wrapped an arm around her waist as she snuggled into his side. A calloused thumb idly caressed the side of her naked breast.

*****

Cecilia nervously checked the belt on her new lightweight spring coat. She'd had to buy a whole new wardrobe to accommodate her ripe new body so this was the first time she'd worn it. She tried to reassure herself that the knee length bright red coat created a perfect foil for her dark brown curls. She'd matched it with a soft, deep gray wrap dress and low black heels. The diamond necklace and earrings from Stan sparkled at her neckline and on her ears. Thinking of Stan, she blushed slightly at the thought of their pre lunch session. He'd penetrated her like he usually did during daytime sessions but didn't allow her to move. Looking up at her with loving eyes, he'd taken slow measured sucks from her breasts while holding her torso to him with strong hands. When he finished, he'd reached up to capture her lips in a deep kiss. Cecilia felt like her heart would burst with love for him. Looking into his lambent blue eyes she'd dropped her forehead to his. "I love you, you know."

He'd smiled triumphantly. "Yes, I do." He paused and cupped the back of her head. Leaning his head to the side he'd whispered in her ear. "I love you more than words can say Mrs. Bergstrom.

With high heels tapping on the hallway of the lobby to the restaurant, Cecilia reveled in the fresh soreness in her nipples and cunt. She enjoyed carrying these reminders of Stan's possession around with her as she went through her day. Unbeknownst to her, at this thought, her eyes darkened to smoldering chocolate pools. As she walked up to the table containing her friends, several judgmental eyes took in her languorous appearance and bee stung lips. It was obvious that she'd recently been kissed at the least, fucked at the most. The group of women all exchanged meaningful looks. Oblivious to their sideways glances, she removed the coat and handed it to the host. Smiling brightly she pulled out her chair and sat down. "It is so nice to see you all!" She exclaimed.

A dead silence followed her exclamation. Then a well coiffed blonde, Blanche, cleared her throat and spoke. "Cecilia…you've changed." The other women tittered at her words.

Cecilia smiled mildly. "Yes, I've put on a few pounds. Stan and I are trying to get pregnant and the doctor said I needed to gain a few pounds in order to enhance my fertility."

The women next to her a skinny red head, oh it was Emily, looked her up and down. "I think I'm actually smaller than you now."

Cecilia smiled at her warmly. "You certainly have lost a lot of weight Emily. I hope it has brought you all you thought it would."

Emily's eyes darkened. "My husband isn't very happy about it." She brightened. "But look…I can now wear this couture dress!" She ran a hand down her side.

Cecilia looked at her ruefully. "You certainly can."

One of the other women, an ebony haired socialite whose name was Sydney broke in. "Your breasts seem disproportionately large compared to the rest of your body." She gasped and looked at Cecilia in excitement. "Did you have them done?"

Cecilia shook her head in bemusement. "Uh…no."

"So why are they so big?" Blanche asked rudely. She looked like a shark moving in on its prey.

Cecilia blushed deep red and looked down at her hands. "We might have to adopt if my gaining weight doesn't work." She paused and took a drink of water. "Stan suggested that we start to stimulate my breasts in order to bring milk in if we have to adopt." She shrugged. "It can take a long time for the breasts to produce sufficient amounts of milk for a baby."

Sydney took a drink of water and made is if to speak then stopped as the waiter arrived to take their order. All of the other women raised their eyebrows at Cecelia's order of a salmon fillet with a side of rice and veggies. She heard a shocked whisper of "Carbs!" as she finished up her order and snapped the menu shut.

Sydney continued as if they hadn't been interrupted. "So, are you using a breast pump then? How often do you have to do it?" She looked around at the circle of shocked faces. "I should warn you that you are absolutely going to ruin your breasts if you go along with this idea." She looked down at her own pert A cup breasts. "I bottle fed all of my children. Look how firm my girls stayed." She looked around the table smugly. They all nodded their heads in agreement at her words.

Cecilia cleared her throat then spoke carefully. "Stan doesn't want me to use a pump so he does it himself."

Dead silence then Blanche spoke in a crackly voice. "So." She cleared her throat. "Your husband…" She seemed at a loss for words.

Cecilia smiled wryly. "My husband sucks on my breasts several times a day." As if they were one person, all of the women at the recoiled at her words.

Emily laid her hand on Cecilia's arm. "Is that awful for you?" Her face reflected concern.

Cecilia shrugged. "Oddly enough, it isn't. I was a little sore at first but now." She stopped. "But now…I like it. It makes me feel closer to him."

Sydney leaned in and whispered. "Are you producing milk yet?"

Cecilia shook her head. "No, but I imagine it will be soon. Stan says that we will increase the amount of stimulation sessions once we know for sure that our adoptive baby is on the way."

All of the women sat back and shook their heads. They all seemed at a loss for words. Finally Emily picked up the conversational thread.

"So, what else have you been up to? We haven't seen you for months."

Cecilia smiled in relief at the change of subject. "I'm volunteering at a low income day care three days a week. I'm also taking cooking lessons and I've started doing embroidery.

She heard a stifled snicker to her left. "Quite the Suzy homemaker." Someone muttered under her breath. Cecilia blushed again.

Blanche started to talk then stopped and smiled up at the waiter as he served her salad. They all waited until they'd been served. As the waiter walked away, Blanche looked back toward Cecilia. "So…it seems like you've turned over a new leaf." A few titters at her words then she continued. "You've never had time to do volunteer work or learn domestic sciences." She stopped and took a small bite of lettuce. After she swallowed she continued. "Your self- care schedule took up most of your time."

Cecilia nodded. "That's true. Stan decided that I needed to cut down the amount of time I spend exercising and the amount of money I spend at the salon. She took a healthy bite of salmon. "He also suggested that I find more worthwhile pursuits to fill my time." She shrugged her shoulders. "I'm enjoying myself and I really don't miss the activities I used to fill my days with."

Sydney broke in. "Is that why your nails are short now?"

Cecilia examined her sensible length manicured nails. "Yes, fake nails and babies don't mix. I can help out a lot more at the daycare now." Shocked silence followed her words.

Emily smiled at her shyly. "I've often thought it would be fun to take cooking lessons."

Cecilia nodded at her. "If you want, I can text you their contact information."

Emily clapped her hands excitedly. "I'd love that…thanks!"

The other women exchanged droll glances. "Better watch out Emily or you'll gain all of the weight back like Cecilia." Blanche warned. The other women muttered in agreement.

Emily looked down then shot a sideways glance at Cecilia. She winked then turned her attention back to the food on her plate.

The rest of the luncheon consisted of desultory conversation among "the skinnies" as Cecilia had dubbed them. She was no longer an interesting topic of conversation so they all ignored her. Finishing up her salmon, she wiped her mouth and drank the last of her glass of water. Smiling around at the ring of stiff faces, she threw her cloth napkin down on her plate. "Got to run." She stood up and signaled the waiter for her check. Looking at it she handed it back to the waiter with a few bills. "You can keep the change." She gathered her coat on the way out of the restaurant. Tears gathered in the corner of her eyes. She impatiently wiped them away as she exited the front door and made her way to her car. Finally sitting in her car, she rested her forehead on the steering wheel for a moment and thought.

She'd experienced a strange sense of déjà vu during her experience in the restaurant. Thinking back five years ago when she'd been a young bride, she'd been treated much in the same fashion by these women. Rather than look for a new group of friends, she'd adapted and became like them. She frowned as she tried to remember why she'd become friends with them in the first place. A light bulb went off in her head. Blanche was an old friend of her mother's and had taken her under her wing when Cecilia was a young newlywed. The invitation to their weekly lunches was considered a major social coup among the upper crust of their town so Cecilia had doggedly held on until she'd become one of them and, in fact, had become the lead bitch. One of them, she snorted, somewhere in the process she'd lost herself and her relationship with her husband.

Sitting up she determinedly wiped the tears from her checks and took out her cell phone. She needed to make some new friends! Briefly searching in her contacts she pressed the call button. The phone rang a few times then was answered. "Hello, this is Sarah."

Cecilia smiled at her bright tone. "Sarah, this is Cecilia. I…I'd like to join your Submissive Wives group.

Chapter Six – Family Ties

"You may experience some disapproval from friends and family when they realize that you've chosen to live a lifestyle involving Domination and submission. One look at your wife's serene countenance will convince you that you've made the right decision."
Excerpt from How to Be a Dominant Husband by Penelope Wiggins

"Do you have everything packed?" Stan dropped a kiss to the top of Cecilia's head as she zipped the last of her suitcases.

Smiling up at him with warm eyes, Cecilia flipped the large suitcase up on end so he could grab the handle. "Yup, all done." She answered.

Stan grabbed her bag and slung it over his shoulder. "We'd better get going then…it's a three hour drive to your parent's home." Cecilia picked up her makeup bag and followed him down the stairs.

The drive ended up taking them almost four hours because Stan accidentally took a wrong turn. By the time they reached Cecilia's home town it was almost time for lunch. Stan looked over at Cecilia in the seat next to him and noted that her breasts looked incredibly engorged. "I think we're going to have to stop somewhere before we drive to your folk's house. You're starting to look really uncomfortable."

Cecilia looked down at her chest and sighed. "I think you're right." She got a sly look in her eye. "I know a place we can go."

After following Cecilia's instructions, Stan ended up driving to a point overlooking Cecilia's hometown. He turned off the car and rotated in his seat to smile at her knowingly. "So, my guess would be that this is the local make out spot for teens?"

Busy unbuttoning her blouse, Cecilia stopped to smile at him in amusement. "You got me Honey. I never spent any time here but I've heard stories…"

Stan laughed. "I guess we will create some memories for you. Shall we retire to the back seat?"

In order to save time, Cecilia and Stan concentrated on relieving the engorged condition of Cecilia's breasts. Stan diligently applied himself to the task while Cecilia straddled him without penetration and caressed his head. They both jumped when a loud knock sounded on the car window. Stan groaned when he saw the police uniform on the man on the outside of the vehicle. He gently set Cecilia aside and scooted over to hit the control to open the window. Cecilia hastily covered up as Stan dealt with the law. "Hello Officer. How may I help you?" Stan smiled engagingly up at the young man in the blue uniform.

Officer Smith, according to his badge, squinted at him through suspicious eyes and looked inside the vehicle as if he thought he'd find some sort of contraband. "Aren't you a little old to be indulging in slap and tickle on Lover's Point?" He inquired with a wicked twinkle in his eye.

Stan cleared his throat and glanced sideways at his wife. "Uh, my wife is attempting to wean our son from breastfeeding but today she became unpleasantly engorged. We don't have a pump with us so I offered to relieve her of her pain." He looked the police officer in the eye. "I was sucking the extra milk out of her breasts when you walked up."

The young police officer pushed his hat to the back of his head and scratched his forehead. "Ahhh...that makes more sense." He leaned forward and rested his forearms on the edge of the window. "I've done that for my wife a time or two as well." He laughed. "We still play a little even though our youngest is now five." He stood up and attempted to reassert his position as an authority figure. "Tell you what, I'll give you another thirty minutes then I'll be coming back up here to kick you out." He winked at them. "Don't worry. No one else will bother you until you are done." With these words he turned on his heels and walked back toward his squad car. Soon he turned started it and drove away from them.

Stan turned back to Cecilia and opened his arms. "We have the stamp of approval from the law. Come over here Darling so I can make you comfortable." Cecilia laughed and settled herself over his lap again.

*****

They turned up at Cecilia's childhood home about an hour later. They knocked on the large door while holding hands and smiling at one another. After a few minutes, the door cracked open. An officious elderly man in a uniform peered out at them from the depths of the shadowy hallway. "Yes?"

Cecilia looked at him hesitantly. "Beatty? It's me Cecilia."

He looked at her myopically through his thick glasses. "Miss Cecee?"

Cecilia smiled happily. "Yes, can we come in?"

He opened the door. "Of course Miss Cecee. Follow me and I'll tell your parents that you're here"

They followed him down the marble lined hallway to the front sitting room. He bowed as he exited the room. Cecilia and Stan took a seat right next to each other on the love seat. They linked hands and waited while exchanging meaningful glances. After a few minutes they heard heavy foot falls punctuated by the staccato tapping of high heel shoes. Cecilia stood up as her parents entered the room. "Daddy!" She rushed over to give the distinguished silver haired man a hug.

He smiled warmly down at his daughter and wrapped her in his arms. "Cecee. I'm so happy to see you darlin'." His voice held a hint of an Irish lilt.

Stan stood up and walked forward with his hand out. "Quinn, nice to see you."

Quinn released his daughter and held out a hand to Stan. "Bergstrom, thanks for bringing our daughter home." They shook hands and exchanged nods.

"Quinn, move so I can see our daughter." An imperious voice ordered from behind his back. Raising his eyebrows in apology, Quinn moved aside so his wife could make her greetings. "Cecilia!" Cecilia's mother, Helen, swept forward dripping in jewelry and haute couture. She stopped short raising a well plucked eyebrow as she took in Cecilia's appearance. "What have you done to yourself?"

Cecilia moved closer to Stan as if seeking support. Smiling down at her reassuringly, he wrapped an arm around her waist and pulled her against his side. Raising melting brown eyes so similar to her mother's, Cecilia managed a wavering smile. "What do you mean Mother?"

Helen sniffed and gave her another up and down look. "It looks like you've gained some weight and your breasts...did you have them done?" Her tone implied that Cecilia was one step away from being a stripper.

Cecilia and Stan exchanged glances. "We're trying to have a baby Mom. The doctor suggested that I gain weight in order to increase my fertility." Cecilia's voice shook a bit while making the explanation. Stan's arm tightened around her waist in silent support.

"And your breasts?"

Cecelia's cheeks bloomed with color. "They just got bigger when I gained weight."

Helen looked at her appraisingly for a moment. "They must ruin the lines of any couture clothing you wear."

Cecelia gathered her composure and lifted her chin. "Actually, I've found couture clothing made for more curvaceous women. As far as my chest, my tailor has been able to make adequate alterations to accommodate it.

Quinn broke in with a warning glance at his wife. "For God's sake woman. Leave the girl alone. She's here five minutes and you're already criticizing her." He looked at Cecelia. "You're absolutely gorgeous, Love. I've never cared for the starving refugee look myself." He shot a telling glare at his fashionably thin wife. Turning back to their guests, he swept his arm toward the doorway of the room. "Speaking of starving, I imagine you are hungry for lunch?"

Stan nodded his head. "Yes Sir. We didn't stop to eat."

Quinn rubbed his hands together. "Well, come on then. I'll have the housekeeper set two more places for you." They all walked companionably down the long hallway to the large dining room. "Helga!" Quinn bellowed as they entered the room.

A stout woman in a black uniform stuck her head through the swinging doors on the side of the room. "Yes Sir?"

"Please set two more places for my daughter and her husband." Quinn ordered as he returned to his abandoned place at the table. Picking up a cloth napkin, he spread it over his lap. "Come on now...sit, sit." He waved his hand at two empty places on one end of the large table. Helen haughtily sat in her place across from Quinn. Stan and Cecilia exchanged glances and took the indicated places.

Helga hurriedly placed silverware and cloth napkins in front of them. "It's so nice to see you Miss Cecilia." She bobbed her graying head at Stan. "Mr. Bergstrom." She stopped to catch her breath. "I can serve you creamy butternut squash soup or a chicken salad." She cut a glance to Stan. "I also have ham and cheese sandwiches Sir."

Stan looked up at Helga. "Please split a sandwich and my wife and myself will each take a half. Cecilia would you also like some soup?" She nodded. "We each will take a bowl of soup as well."

Helen looked at them with narrowed eyes as Helga exited the room. "Since when does he order for you Cecilia? And when did you start eating carbs?"

Cecilia shrugged her shoulders and attempted to look unconcerned. "I like it when Stan is in charge. And as far as your last question, I'm not restricting my diet as much anymore."

Stan reached over and laced his fingers in hers again. "Cecee was teetering on the edge of having an eating disorder. She's asked me to help her eat a healthy amount of food." He held up her hand and kissed the backs of her fingers. "As you can see, the results are breath taking."

Helen took a breath as if to continue interrogating her daughter. Quinn shot her a warning look and she subsided in a huff. The room fell into silence while Helga served Stan and Cecilia. The two of them each picked up a sandwich and took a bite. "Oh…" Cecilia looked at Stan. "It doesn't have mustard. I'll go get some for you." She jumped up and threw the napkin on the table. She swept out of the room through the swinging doors to the industrial sized kitchen.

Helga turned to her in shock. "Miss Cecilia?"

Cecilia smiled at her. "Stan likes stone ground mustard. Is there any in the refrigerator?" Too shocked to speak, Helga simply nodded and pointed at the stainless steel refrigerator in the corner. Cecilia briskly walked over to it and grabbed a small jar of mustard. She also grabbed a bottle of sparkling water from the beverage cooler. Pushing her way back through the swinging doors, Cecilia placed the mustard and the bottled water on the table by her husband's plate.

Stan grabbed her hand and kissed her palm. "Thanks Love." Cecilia smiled at him as she regained her seat. Looking at the other occupants of the table, she met two pairs of shocked eyes.

Helen cleared her throat. "Uh, we have servants for that. You don't need to wait on Stan. "

Cecilia smiled brightly at her parents. "I don't mind. I like taking care of my husband." Helen's eyebrow raised but she made no further comment.

*****

After lunch, Stan and Cecilia retired to their room to freshen up and rest. Quinn had suggested that they all go to the country club that evening for dinner. They'd readily agreed but thought that they would need naps in order to be fresh enough for an evening out. A servant had brought up their suitcases and had unpacked them for them so all they had to do was undress and climb into the sumptuous bed. Stan wrapped his arms around Cecilia and lightly kissed the side of her head. "Sleep for a bit Hon. We'll need our energy for running the gauntlet tonight at the country club." Smiling at his humorous tone, Cecilia slipped into a light slumber. She woke up a bit later to the sensation of Stan gently sucking on her left breast. Wrapping her hands around the back of his head, she sleepily smoothed his hair as he stimulated the nipple. Stan disengaged from the breast and lifted his head to fix her with a navy blue gaze. "Hey sleepyhead. I figured that we'd better do this before dinner so you aren't in too much discomfort."

Cecilia smiled down at him lovingly as he gently shifted her onto her side. She automatically held up the right breast for him until he was positioned correctly. After he started suckling, she drifted back into sleep. When she woke up again, Stan was fast asleep with his head resting upon her chest. Both of her breasts felt soft so she knew that he'd finished his ministrations before he succumbed to sleep. Breathing a sigh of relief, she looked over to the clock. In sudden alarm she started shaking Stan's shoulder. "Stan, Stan…it's time to get up." His blond eyelashes fluttered as his eyes opened. Pale blue eyes looked up at her in a daze for a second and then warmed.

"Good evening Darling." His hand rubbed up and down her side then tangled in her hair. Rolling between her legs, he rubbed the head of his cock up and down on her rapidly moistening slit. "Pull your knees to your chest Hon." Cecilia sleepily complied smiling at him with velvet brown eyes. Stan took her in one deep thrust then stopped for a moment to look into her eyes. "I love you." He positioned her legs around his waist and wrapped the other hand under her head. With eyes locked, they rocked together. Stan leaned over and took her lips in a deep kiss. His tongue mimicked the movement of his cock in and out. After a few deep thrusts, Cecilia felt her orgasm roll from deep inside of her. As she arched back with closed eyes, her cunt clamped down on his penis. Stan groaned as he filled her with his seed. He dropped his forehead on top of hers. Cecilia's muscular sheath rippled around his penis as she came down. Stan combed her hair back from her forehead with his fingers. "Thank you." He dropped a chaste kiss on her lips.

*****

Dinner at the country club was less dinner and more an opportunity to see and be seen. Helen led her family around to meet all of the people she deemed worth greeting. Always a master of the spin, she explained away Cecilia's voluptuous figure with the sly insinuation that she might be pregnant. Much to Cecilia's relief, a hostess finally seated them at their table. After looking at the menu, all of the members of their party ordered dinner then indulged in small talk. Cecilia gave a heartfelt mental groan when she saw Blaine's parents bearing down on them. Amy and Dexter Madison arrived at their table with big smiles and handshakes. Amy wasted no time in getting to the point. "So Cecilia, we hear from Blaine that you've been very busy lately. He says you hardly have time to check your Facebook page." Amy looked at her with an inquisitive face then glanced briefly at Stan with suspicious eyes.

Cecilia mentally rolled her eyes. Crap! Just what she needed. "Uh, I've decided to take on more lessons and volunteer activities lately. I just haven't had the time to spend on social media."

Amy started to speak, stopped, glanced at Stan then back at Cecilia. "Uh, he's been a little worried about you...that you might not be allowed to go on-line." She paused meaningfully.

Cecilia laughed then looked up at them. "I've recently decided that I needed to spend my time on more worthwhile pursuits than social media. I only check my computer a few times a week now."

Amy looked at her closely. "Okay, I just wanted to check in. You can contact me at any time if you need any help." With these words she crooked a finger at her husband and they walked away.

There was a dead silence at their table then Quinn cleared his throat. "So, you're taking lessons and volunteering now?" He directed the question at Cecilia.

She nodded gratefully. "I'm taking cooking classes. I took needlework classes and I'm volunteering at a low income daycare three days a week now."

Helen looked at her in horror. "Aren't you afraid of catching something from those...children?"

The corner of Cecilia's mouth lifted. "Maybe at first. Now I enjoy holding the babies and thinking of the day I'll be holding my own." She reached over to grasp her husband's hand.

Quinn's eyes passed back and forth between the two of them as a wrinkle appeared between his eyebrows. Conversation came to a halt as their dinner appeared and they began to eat. Helen managed to hold her tongue as Stan prompted Cecilia to eat more of the food on her plate. After they'd all eaten and the plates were removed, Stan turned to his wife and held out his hand. "Dance?" Eager for the opportunity to escape her parents' scrutiny, Cecilia scooted out of the booth and allowed Stan to lead her to the dance floor. Since it was a slow, romantic tune Stan pulled her close in his arms and began to deftly guide her around the room. "So...tell me about this...Blaine."

Cecilia started at his words and leaned back to look him in the eyes warily. "Uh, I went to prep school with him. We've been friends ever since."

Stan's arms tightened around her waist. "So, why would he feel worried about your safety?" His mild tone held a bit of steel.

Cecilia shivered at his tone. Oddly, her nipples came to rock hard points. "Uh, I told him that you'd restricted my computer time."

Stan's lips pressed together. "Exactly how close are you to this boy?" His blue eyes lightened to a wintry tint as they locked on her wide chocolate orbs.

Dark color climbed up Cecilia's cheeks. "We've been friends for years. In the last few years we've talked a lot on Facebook. He was used to seeing me online at least once a day until you restricted my computer use." She paused. "He was concerned when I told him the reason why I couldn't talk to him as much as I used to." Her voice trailed off.

Stan's fingers bit into her waist. "Was there any sort of…inappropriate contact between you two?"

Cecilia's head dropped to his chest. "Not really." She muttered against the fine material of his suit.

Hard fingers lifted her chin so guilty brown eyes could meet angry blue ones. "Explain."

She took a deep breath. "Well, I may have talked to him a little bit about…our relationship and the things I didn't like about you." She hastened to add. "I am very happy in our relationship now."

Stan's jaw hardened. "So you were telling this boy the things you should have been saying to me? That could be considered emotional infidelity." His quiet voice radiated with anger.

Cecilia dropped her head in shame. "I know. I'm sorry." She lifted her face to look pleadingly at him. "I swear that there hasn't been any inappropriate contact since we…renewed our relationship."

Stan's grip on her waist loosened. "That's good." He stopped dancing and looked down at her. "Unfortunately, I think that I'm going to have punish you for this. You were leading that boy on and you were lying to me by omission." He grasped her shoulders and gave her a small shake. "Do you understand?"

Cecilia nodded her still down turned head. "Yes Sir." Her voice trailed off and she grasped his sleeve urgently as she turned up beseeching eyes. "Can you do it now so I don't have to anticipate it for the rest of the night?"

Stan's face softened. "Is there a place we can go where we can have some privacy and so no one can hear us?"

Cecilia thought for a moment with a furrowed brow. "I know the perfect place." She grabbed Stan's hand and led him back to her parent's table. "Dad, Mom…I'm going to show Stan the grounds outside. We'll be back soon." She smiled at them with fever bright eyes.

Quinn's shrewd eyes flitted back and forth between the two of them. "Okay darlin'. Your mother and I will be here when you get back." Helen gave them an absent wave as she checked text messages on her smart phone.

Cecilia and Stan picked their way through the crowd to the large, open glass doors leading to a wide patio. Cecilia led Stan down the stairs out to a flagstone pathway. They walked through the dimly lit garden taking progressively smaller paths until they arrived at a small stone structure with tiny marble columns in front. Cecilia walked up the steps and tried the handle. It was locked. She jiggled the door and knocked. Not a noise from the inside. She turned to Stan with a shy smile. "I think this will work. No one is here."

Stan placed his hands in his front pockets and rocked back on his heels. "That's all fine and well, Hon, but how are we going to get in?"

Cecelia smiled at him wickedly. "You have to remember that I spent a large portion of my childhood coming to this club. I know a few secrets." She walked over to lift up an innocuous looking rock in the rock bed around the house. Turning over the rock, she gave a cry of triumph as she lifted up a large brass key. "Here it is!" She walked over to the door and inserted the lock into the keyhole. The door opened smoothly. They walked into a dark room. Cecilia fumbled around on the wall next to the door. Light filled the room after she found the switch. Stan stopped short behind her. The room was scattered with an assortment of furniture in no particular order. A few boxes were stacked against a far wall. "I think this was some sort of guest home when the country club was a private residence years ago." Cecelia turned around to close and lock the door. "Now they store furniture and other items here." She lifted her eyebrows wickedly. "It was a great make out spot when I was a teenager."

Stan regarded her steadily. "You seem to be quite an expert on the make out spots in your home town."

His dry tone wasn't lost on Cecelia. She walked over to stand in front of him and placed her hands on his chest in supplication. "I didn't go all the way with them Stan. If it makes any difference to you, I only had sex with one guy before I met you."

Stan lifted his hands up to tightly grasp her upper arms. "Was it Blaine?" His voice came out in a low growl.

Cecilia let out a trill of laughter. At the warning light in Stan's eyes she smothered the laugh. He didn't find any of this amusing. "No, it was my college boyfriend. We only did it a few times and I didn't find it all that satisfying." Her voice trailed off and a pink tinge touched her cheeks. "Then I met you..."

Stan gathered her against his chest. "And…"

She sighed contentedly against his chest. "And…it was, is very satisfying."

Stan's large hand smoothed up and down her back. "So, what happened to us? Why were we at odds for the last few years?"

Cecilia turned away from him and wrapped her arms around her middle. "I'm not sure. I think it was partly the influence of my friends and my mother. They seemed so disapproving of their husbands. And you…and you didn't seem to want to attend any of the social functions they thought were important." Her voice trailed off. "I thought that maybe you were ashamed to be seen with me so I started to diet so I'd look like them. Losing weight didn't help and, in fact, you seemed annoyed with me all of the time." She turned to him with tears in her eyes. "I was so unhappy and started to have difficulty curbing my tongue. Everyone irritated me, especially you."

Stan looked at her for a moment with searching eyes. "This is going to seem like an odd question but when did you start missing your period?"

Cecilia stopped for a moment, then looked at him in amazement. "About the time I started feeling irritated by everyone. "

Stan nodded sagely. "That's what I thought." He sighed heavily. "Listen Cecilia, I didn't tell you this before but you know the book I gave you?"

She frowned. "How to Be a Submissive Wife?"

He nodded. "Yes…uh I e-mailed the author about two weeks into our agreement. I felt like I needed help in re-establishing emotional intimacy in our marriage and I thought she might be able to help." He stopped for a moment and pinched the bridge of his nose between two fingers. "She, uh, called me and we discussed strategies to improve our marriage." He turned towards Cecilia and placed both hands on the top of her shoulders. "One thing she mentioned is that painfully thin women often don't have sufficient amounts of female sex hormones, especially progesterone." He continued. "She said that progesterone is the 'get along' hormone. If a woman doesn't have enough progesterone, she'll be very difficult to live with." He coughed. "Similar to the phenomenon experienced by women and their spouses during menopause."

Cecilia's eyes opened in shock. "So when I gained weight and got my cycle back…"

Stan smiled. "Your hormones leveled out. That is one of the reasons why you've been more content in the last few months."

Cecilia's brow furrowed. "And the other reasons…?"

Stan cleared his throat. "Well, the nipple stimulation helps as well." He admitted.

"What?" She questioned.

"She, we decided that you needed help in bonding. Nipple stimulation stimulates the release of a hormone called oxytocin. Oxytocin increases bonding among partners and creates a sense of well being in the woman." He looked at her apprehensively while revealing this information. He continued in a rush. "It will also be quite helpful if we do decide to adopt a baby."

Cecilia spoke slowly. "So you knowingly manipulated my hormones in order to control me?"

Stan rushed to her side. "I wanted to save our marriage." He grabbed her arms. "I love you and I couldn't stand letting you go."

She looked up at him. "How about the domestic discipline?"

A slight blush settled on his blade like cheekbones. "I wanted to reassert control and have the means by which to help you. You know that you wouldn't have made the necessary changes unless I was in charge." He looked pleadingly in her eyes. "You have to admit that submitting to me as the head of the household has led to many positive changes in your life." He smiled wickedly. "And you're having some of the best orgasms of your life."

She blushed at his words and dropped her head. Stan shook her slightly. "Right?" She muttered something under her breath. Stan leaned over next to her downturned head. "What?"

"I said yes Sir." She muttered.

Stan sighed in relief. "So, wife, are you ready for your punishment?" Cecilia nodded her downturned head. Stan looked around the room for something to use as a spanking implement. Finally he sighed and unlooped his belt from his pants. "It looks like I'll have to use this." At Cecilia's alarmed look he hastened to reassure her. "Don't worry. I won't swing it very hard." Then in a hard voice he ordered. "Expose your breasts then lean over the back of that chaise longue." Cecilia automatically shimmied her shoulder straps down over her arms and released the clasps on the bra to expose her pendulous breasts. Stan stepped up in front of her and rubbed a calloused thumb over her rock hard nipples. "I've changed my mind. Grab the back of the chaise with your hands and lean over. I want to see these beauties swing during your punishment." Cecilia complied by leaning over and grasping the back of the piece of furniture with one hand while lifting her skirt to expose her naked ass with the other. Knowing that Stan like to look at her pussy while he spanked her, she shifted her legs apart far enough to expose her glistening pink cunt to his gaze. After she'd positioned herself to his preferences, she grabbed the top of the chaise with the second hand and braced herself on her high heel clad feet.

Stan lifted the doubled over belt then stopped for a moment to admire her beauty. Her mink brown hair was piled on top of her head in a simple chignon with wispy ends straggling over the sides of her face and down her neck. His gaze moved up her body to settle appreciatively on the heavy, blue veined breasts dangling down from her small frame. Her dark brown, puffy nipples stuck down at least an inch as the breasts gently swayed. It gave Stan a thrill to know that he had wrought this transformation in his formerly petite bride. No one could doubt that she belonged to him after seeing his handiwork. He walked behind her to continue his inspection. Her widespread legs revealed swollen dark pink inner pussy lips with an engorged clitoris peeking out from between them. Female arousal juices were already coating her cunt lips and had started to slick down her thighs. She might act outraged at his high handedness but he could see the truth in her body's reaction. She enjoyed submitting to his domination. With this confirmation that he was on the right track, Stan raised the doubled over belt. "I'll do a few light slaps to warm you up then I'll give you ten good ones. Are you ready?'

A small voice came from Cecilia's lowered head. "Yes Sir."

"Swack!" Cecilia's hips cringed at the first blow but she held herself in position. Stan continued with a few more warm up slaps. Once her ass was a light pink, Stan continued in earnest. He laid into her with a smack over her right butt cheek. He could see the red outline of the belt on her flesh. She moaned as her full breasts bounced back and forth. Stan gave her five more, alternating cheeks with each swat. Cecilia's face was bright red when Stan checked in on her. He could see tears gathering in the corners of her eyes.

Good! He finished up with four hard smacks including the creases of her thighs. Cecilia jerked at these final corrections but stayed in place. Stan rubbed her butt soothingly. "You're all done Darling. You did very well." Cecilia sobbed silently. He gathered her into his arms and rocked back and forth while she cried. After she quieted he leaned back and cleaned the tears off of her cheeks with his thumb and then his handkerchief. "Do you understand why I punished you?" He asked quietly.

Through hitching breaths, Cecilia answered him. "I was inappropriately close to another man." She sniffed then continued. "And I led him on."

Stan nodded his head. "That's right." He gathered her close again and spoke into the top of her head. "All is forgiven Love." They rocked for a moment.

Stan dropped his mouth next to her ear to whisper. "I want you right now. Go and kneel on all fours on top of the chaise. I want your upper body held down close enough for your nipples to touch the fabric while I fuck you from behind." She pulled out of his arms and turned to ready herself for his possession. Stan caught her arm. "And Cecilia, you don't get to come this time. This is to establish that you are mine and that I control everything in your life including your orgasms...do you understand?" He lifted her chin in a hard hand. Blushing with downcast eyes she nodded again. Without a word she climbed on top of the wide chaise on all fours. Reaching back she flipped the skirt up and out of the way again over her back. After exposing her cunt for his use, she settled down on her elbows at the right angle to rub her nipples on the seat of the chaise. Stan wasted no time in unzipping his pants and pulling out his throbbing member. Knowing that his penetration would be especially deep in this position, Stan climbed up on the chaise, rubbed his swollen cockhead over her wet lips and positioned it just barely in the entrance of her vagina. Without any warning, he grabbed both of her hip bones and drilled straight into her pussy with one hard thrust. He heard a muffled Umph! from Cecilia at his rough penetration. Her moist channel fluttered around his invader as if to adjust itself to his size. As he withdrew and hammered in again, he could feel his penis hit her cervix. A shuddering moan came from Cecilia at this deep penetration. Stan grinned to himself at the stimulation she must be receiving from her sensitive nipples grazing the rough fabric on the chaise along with the sting she felt every time his hips slapped her sore ass. Being fucked this deep was also a turn on for her. She liked a little pain with her sex. Grinning evilly he started a hard driving rhythm making sure to slap her sore cheeks every time with his hips. Just as he felt Cecelia starting to ramp up to orgasm, he groaned and emptied himself into her passive body. As he came he muttered the word that had been running through his head since he'd heard about her relationship with Blaine. "Mine!" Though she hadn't come, at his words, Cecilia's muscular passage sucked every bit of cum it could into her womb. Stan wondered if he'd finally made her pregnant with this interlude. Groaning at the clutch of her warm cunt, he pulled out with a spill of their commingled fluids. Wiping himself off with his handkerchief, Stan stood up and pulled her to standing as well. He could see their mingled juices running down her legs. "I'll wipe off your thighs but I don't want you to clean my cum off of your pussy until we get back to the house." He lifted her chin to look into her flushed face. "Do you understand?"

    Cecilia mutinously set her chin. "Yes Sir." She held up her skirt and widened her legs so he could wipe her thighs. The smell of their joining permeated the air as she opened her legs. Stan sniffed appreciatively as he attended to cleaning his wife. Once he was finished with her thighs, Stan folded up the handkerchief and placed it in his pocket. His attention shifted to the two naked, swollen breasts currently standing to attention under his gaze. Locking eyes with Cecilia, he hefted both breasts in his hands while running his thumbs over the nipples. Cecilia winced at how sensitive they now were from their rubbing on the nubby fabric of the chaise.

    "Poor babies." He crooned. "I think they need some soothing." Ignoring Cecilia's objections, he lowered his head to delicately lick one long nipple then the other. Both traitorous tips hardened at his attentions. Groaning deep in his throat, he captured one breast in his mouth and sucked deeply. Cecelia winced at his suction. She was really sore! Suddenly her hips started undulating against Stan's thigh. Oh no...she couldn't believe that she was getting turned on again. While she was attempting to stave off an orgasm, Stan suddenly released the breast and looked at her in surprise. "I felt some fluid come out in my mouth. I think your milk is coming in!" They shared expressions of mingled alarm and delight. Stan reached down to squeeze her other breast. His eyebrows raised at the tiny droplets of white fluid that formed in response to his stimulation. "Yep, that looks like milk!" He looked up at her in askance. "Did you bring any breast pads?"

She shook her head in alarm. "I didn't think I'd need them." Her voice trailed off.

He squeezed her in his arms. "Don't worry, tomorrow we'll say we need to do a little sightseeing and pick some up when we're out and about."

Cecilia shook her head. "That is the least of my worries. I'm making milk and I don't have a baby yet. What are we going to do?"

Stan looked at her in puzzlement. "What we've always been doing. I don't mind getting a little milk in my mouth occasionally. At this point in our relationship I think the benefits definitely outweigh the risks of continuing." He gathered her in his arms with her leaking breasts squashed between the two of them. "I love the time we spend together stimulating your nipples. I don't want to give that up."

Cecilia looked up at him shyly. "Me neither." She admitted. They hugged and kissed. Before returning to her parents, Stan suckled on both of Cecilia's breasts drawing out all of the milk he could. They didn't want to shock her parents with wet spots over her nipples! After restoring themselves to a semblance of normalcy, the two of them strolled back into the dining room of the country club. Most members had finished dinner and were now visiting and dancing. Pasting smiles on their faces, the couple returned to Cecilia's parents' table. Quinn's appraising eyes ran up and down their forms as if he could see that something had shifted between them. His gaze lingered for a long time on Cecilia's flushed cheeks. His eyebrows rose almost to his hairline when he noted Cecilia's slight wince as she sat down at the table. Anger filled his gaze until he noted the loving glances occurring between his formerly brittle daughter and her husband. His hand tightened around the rocks glass he held. Later tonight he'd get some answers!

*****

After they returned back to Cecilia's parents' home, both of the women begged fatigue and went to their bedrooms. Quinn and Stan stood for a moment and looked at each other. "Want to play some pool?" Quinn inquired.

Stan shrugged his shoulders. "Sounds good to me." They walked companionably to the large game room in the back of the house. Stan admired the relaxed masculine air of the space.

Quinn talked over his shoulder as he poured himself a drink. "Only place I forbid Helen to touch when we built this place." He walked back to Stan and took a small drink. "I need to have at least one room I can relax in completely." Raising his eyebrows, he lifted the glass. "Drink?"

Stan responded as he chose a pool cue. "Sure. I'll rack them while you get it."

They played in a comfortable silence for quite awhile. Each of them took small sips from their glasses and seemed to enjoy the peace and quiet. Finally Quinn took a drink and cleared his throat. "So, what have you done with my daughter?"

Stan stopped while chalking the cue stick. "What do you mean?" He demurred.

Quinn fixed him with a no nonsense look. "Don't pretend like she isn't different. She's happier, more content. She's a normal weight and seems less obsessed with her appearance in general." He placed both hands on the side of the pool table and leaned forward. "I also noticed that she seemed to be in pain when she sat down tonight after you two disappeared."

Stan winced and looked away while rubbing his chin. "Listen Sir, I can explain." He took a deep breath. "Before the holidays last year Cecilia and I went out to dinner with a few of my employees." He looked up at Quinn. "You know how she could be…brittle, insulting." He shook his head. "She was in great form that night, making one of the women break out in tears at her insults." He got a small smile on his face. "The wife of one of my other employees defended her. Her husband took her off soon after and I followed them." He shook his head. "I was curious what was up with them. It was obvious he was calling the shots and she was letting him." He smiled sideways at Quinn. "It was also obvious that they'd rekindled the romance in their marriage. They couldn't keep their hands off of each other. So, needless to say, I wanted to know what they were going to do. I saw them both disappear into a handicapped restroom in the back of the restaurant. I walked back and stood next to the door and listened." He smiled ruefully. "I have to admit that I thought I'd hear an argument or maybe sex sounds. Instead I heard the obvious slapping noises you would hear if someone was being spanked. I could also hear his wife counting the spanks as he administered them. When he was done punishing her I could hear them talking and then silence. After a few minutes his wife opened the door looking quite flustered when she saw me standing there. After she scurried back to join our party, I took her husband, Joe, aside and we talked for a few moments at the bar." He looked far into space and twisted the pool cue around in his hands. "Joe told me about a set of companion books he and his wife had read. One was called How to Be a Submissive Wife and the other one was called How to Be a Dominant Husband. His wife had requested this change in their marriage after reading the first book. After experiencing some of the benefits of having a submissive wife he was hooked and began to act as the head of household." He cleared his throat and stopped.

Quinn broke in. "So you decided to try this yourself?"

Stan nodded. "I downloaded How to Be a Dominant Husband onto my e-reader that evening. After reading it I realized there was no way I'd be able to get Cecilia to voluntarily engage in a domestic discipline marriage...so I figured out a way to coerce her into it." He looked at Quinn with a shamefaced expression. "I'm not proud to admit it but I threatened her with divorce if she didn't comply with my demands and acknowledge me as the head of the household." He shrugged his shoulders. "I was surprised she went along with it, I thought she'd tell me to go to hell and leave."

Quinn gave a shout of laughter at Stan's words. "I doubt she'd do that. When I saw her turning into a wee bitch like her mum, I told her she'd only get a small stipend if you divorced her. There's no way that girl would live without money."

Stan gave a slow nod. "That makes sense now. I was surprised when she submitted to me so quickly." He sighed deeply. "So we started a domestic discipline marriage. I set up the rules. Most of them dealt with her gaining weight and taking on worthwhile pursuits. With a few well timed spankings, she was well on the way to mending her ways. She gained weight and even managed to be polite to most people most of the time...but." He stopped and turned to Quinn with a pleading look in his eyes. "We just didn't have the emotional intimacy that I craved. Spanking, pardon me sir, made her hot and she was always up for intimate relations but she didn't like to cuddle and refused to meet my eyes when we made love. I knew something just wasn't quite right so I e-mailed the author of the two marital self help books I mentioned earlier. You can imagine my surprise when she called me after the holiday season." He rubbed a finger over the side of his nose. "After talking to me, she suggested I try an extreme measure to solidify the emotional bond with Cecilia. She suggested that I enforce nipple stimulation as part of my demands as the head of the household."

Quinn recoiled. "Nipple stimulation? Like what?"

Stan smiled. "I had the same reaction. She suggested that I suck on Cecilia's nipples for at least ten minutes each side five to eight times a day. This type of stimulation helps to increase a hormone related to bonding."

Quinn snorted. "That explains the bigger breasts. Can't that make her lactate over time?"

Stan looked a little ill. "Well supposedly it takes a lot for a women who hasn't been pregnant to start lactating. So far the only thing we've seen is how her breasts get engorged before a nipple stimulation session is due." And a little milk tonight he silently added. He returned to the conversation with his father-in-law. "All I can say is that I saw a major improvement in her demeanor on all levels when we started this regimen. She relaxed in my presence and would even cuddle with me. She was happy to see me and…submission to my position as the head of the household came naturally to her after we started the regular sessions." He shook his head and lifted it up to meet Quinn's eyes. There was a sheen of moisture over his usually icy blue orbs. "My sweet, submissive wife is back."

Quinn looked at him steadily for a moment. "And tonight when she winced?"

Stan's lips firmed. "I found out tonight that she'd been cheating on me emotionally with that boy, Blaine. You remember that his parents stopped by to inquire after her welfare? That was all at the prompting of Blaine. Apparently the two of them have been hot and heavy on Facebook in the last few years."

Quinn's face also tightened. "That boy is incredibly manipulative and lazy. I'm glad that you've blocked his advances. My girl has to know you are worth ten of him."

Stan smiled ruefully. "So maybe now you can understand why I felt the need to give her a punishment spanking. She was emotionally cheating on me and she was leading that boy along."

Quinn nodded slowly. "I don't blame you. You don't want her thinking she can get away with things like that." He looked thoughtful for a moment. "I'm interested in this concept of a domestic discipline marriage." He gave a short bark of laughter. "There's no way Helen would voluntarily enter such an arrangement but now you've got me thinking." He stroked his chin. "We have an infidelity clause in our pre-nuptial contract." He smiled at Stan. "Though you wouldn't believe it, I'm the one who came into this marriage with money. I felt the need for a pre-nup. Helen thought that including the infidelity clause would pay me back for my requiring a pre-nup." The smile turned rueful. "The only other lover I've had is my right hand. Helen on the other hand..." His eyes turned grim. "I know for a fact she's cheated on me with at least three different men." He shrugged. "Like I care. Who wants to bed that bony shrew?" He looked at Stan with a knowing grin. "I did make sure that she's now always followed by a private investigator. I have lots of evidence of her infidelity. I could probably use it to force her into a domestic discipline relationship." He paused for a moment. "I might also enforce the nipple stimulation schedule too. It'd serve her right to start lactating after refusing to breast feed her own child."

Stan looked at him in alarm. "You need to understand that taking on a nipple stimulation schedule is a huge commitment for both parties. If you decide to do five sessions a day you have to do five sessions a day. If you miss a session, your wife will be very uncomfortable. And, if for some reason, she starts to produce milk you will become even more necessary for her comfort unless you are comfortable with her using a breast pump or a surrogate partner." He paused for a moment. "In some ways, it is like bondage for both partners. You can't ever travel too far from one another and you have to keep up to a regular schedule in order for it to work."

Quinn rubbed his hands together in glee. "I've always looked for a way to keep Helen in check. I think this might be the answer. I doubt any of her boy toys would be willing to relieve her if she gets engorged."

Stan looked at him grimly. "It cuts both ways. Make sure that you are ready to be with her so much before you institute the nipple stimulation regimen."

Quinn locked eyes with him for a moment and sharply nodded his understanding. "Okay." He stopped for a moment. "I'm glad that you've managed to make such a connection with my girl. I think my grandchildren will benefit from having a mom who's interested in actually raising them." He stuck out his hand. "Thanks." Stan saw tears glistening in his eyes. They shook hands and returned to their pool game.

Chapter Seven – Sinking Deeper

"Speaking with other like minded woman will help your wife adapt herself to the Domestic Discipline lifestyle." Excerpt from How to Be a Dominant Husband by Penelope Wiggins

    Cecilia nervously ran her hands down the front of her dress as she prepared for her first meeting with the members of the Submissive Wives Club. Sarah had contacted her last week with a meeting date and time. "It should be fun. We have quite a few new members." She burbled. "I'm actually listed as an official group leader on the How to Be a Submissive Wife website." Cecilia took a deep breath. Whoa. She wasn't sure if she'd be comfortable admitting to other women that she enjoyed submitting to her husband's dominion. Remembering the breast pads she'd placed in her bra early in the day, she had to admit that her husband now dominated all aspects of her life. Picking up her purse she took one last look in the mirror. Her breasts now stood out prominently from her small ribcage with distinct nipples pushing against the sturdy fabric of her bra. She was glad that Stan had drained them over lunch time so she'd be comfortable during the meeting. Sighing in resignation she pulled her keys out of her handbag. Time to meet the other submissive wives!

*****

    Sarah welcomed her with a big hug. "Cecilia, you look fantastic! Come on into the living room and meet the other ladies." Cecilia followed her and hesitantly stood in the entryway surveying the group. To her surprise, she saw a few familiar faces. Emily from her lunch group was there and…Stacy from Tiny Sprouts Daycare. Go figure! Pasting a smile on her face, she entered the room with panache. She sat on the couch between Stacy and Emily.
    Reaching over to grab a slice of cucumber off of the plate on the coffee table she turned to face one friend and then the other.

"Who'd figure that we'd all end up here?" Both women broke out laughing. Cecilia joined them after a moment.

Sarah walked into the room and laughed with them. "Well, it looks like we should get this meeting started soon." She sat in an armchair and folded her hands in her lap." Looking around the room gravely she said. "Hi, my name is Sarah and I am a submissive wife."

The other women chimed in and said. "Hi Sarah."

Sarah continued speaking. "It has been almost a year since I made the decision to submit to my husband Joe. Our marriage and my life have improved immeasurably since we took this step." She took a deep breath. "Most of you know my story so I would like to cede the floor to one of our new members." She motioned towards Cecilia and the women sitting on either side of her. "Would you ladies like to share tonight?"

The three exchanged glances then Emily cleared her throat. "I'll start if that is okay." At their approving nods she continued. "My name is Emily and I am a submissive wife. I've been submissive to my husband for the last four months. In fact..." She looked toward Cecilia. "In some ways I was inspired to pursue this path by Cecilia. She attended a society luncheon a few months ago. It was obvious at the luncheon that she'd submitted to her husband's wishes in many matters." She paused. "It was also obvious that she was so much more self confident and serene than before." She added in a smaller voice. "I wanted that for myself." Cecilia reached over to pat her hand.

Sarah smiled at Emily and prompted. "So, in what ways do you submit to your husband?"

Emily blushed and looked down at her hands. "Well, I am available to him sexually at all times." She swallowed nervously. "And I'm not allowed to diet anymore. He doesn't like it when I'm too skinny." She looked around at the group helplessly then continued. "He spanks me if I break any of his rules." She blushed deeply. "The weird part is that I like it all. I'm ready for sex whenever he wants it." She shook her head. "I thought I was a liberated woman until we started this lifestyle. Now I'm happy to let him be in charge." She subsided in obvious embarrassment until she heard the approving applause of the other women then she brightened and sat up straighter.

Stacy looked around and cleared her throat. "I guess that I'll speak next. My name is Stacy and I am a submissive wife." After the group's greetings died down she continued. "First of all, my husband and I started our relationship off with a dominant and submissive element so I've been a submissive wife for seven years." She looked around at the group. "When I decided to take over the foundation that administers the non-profit run by my husband's family I realized that I needed some way to blow off steam from all of that responsibility." She took a breath. "This was when we decided to take our relationship a bit further in the evenings and weekends when we are home." She smiled ruefully. "Now when we are home alone, I take on the role of my husband's slave or his pet. This means that once I walk through the door, I strip down naked, put on my collar and wait for my husband on my knees by the door until he comes home." Cecilia looked sideways at her in surprise. She never would have guessed! Stacy continued. "When he comes home I rise up on my knees and open my mouth to receive his cock. If I'm lucky, he will allow me to worship it for awhile. Often times he will just rest it on my bottom lip then pull it out and zip up. Once he's greeted me, he attaches a leash to my collar and leads me to the bedroom. I crawl on all fours at his side." She smiled around at the group and continued. "Depending on his mood, he might take me or make me wait on a pillow in the corner while he changes from his work clothing. Sometimes he will perform a maintenance spanking with a slipper." She smiled ruefully and continued. "Once he's changed, he leads me to the kitchen where he allows me to stand in order to set the table for him and bring out the food our housekeeper has prepared. Once the food is served, I once again sit on the floor next to his feet and he feeds me. Occasionally, he asks me to give him head while he is eating." She blushed slightly. "After dinner, I'm allowed to stand in order to clear the dirty dishes. When I'm done, I must come to him where ever he is and bow down on the ground with my arms extended waiting for his orders. It is at this time he will often insert a butt plug. The rest of the evening is spent cuddling while we watch television. I may be allowed to worship his cock if he is in the mood. He often plays with my body until bedtime. At bedtime he will usually take me. Sometimes he allows me to come if I've been very good." She stopped for a moment then continued. "Handing over the reins to my husband gives me a break from being in charge at work." She looked around at the group uncertainly. All she saw were approving nods and a few of the ladies clapped.

"Sounds like the two of you have set up a mutually satisfying arrangement." Sarah smiled at Stacy. "Do you ever have trouble submitting?"

Stacy nodded her head and a slight blush tinged her cheeks. "The punishment I hate the most is when he makes me wear the largest butt plug. It hurts so much going in and I feel so full." Her head dropped. "Sometimes he has to spank me in order to make me submit to the insertion of the plug." She heaved a great sigh. "I'm just glad he doesn't use it very often."

Many of the women present nodded their heads knowingly. "During those moments of rebellion, you must remind yourself that your body is your husband's to do with as he wishes. If he feels that you need the reminder of a large plug then you must submit to his wishes." Sarah kindly gazed at Stacy with warm blue eyes as she spoke.

Stacy pursed her lips and then nodded her head. "You are right of course. I'll remind myself of that next time he punishes me."

Sarah smiled at her. "Good." She turned to Cecilia. "So Cecilia, would you like to share with the group?"

Cecilia looked around nervously and then looked down at her hands. "My name is Cecilia and I am a submissive wife." She waited on their greetings. "I submitted to my husband about six months ago when he gave me an ultimatum. Either I accepted his dominion as the head of the household or he was going to divorce me." She looked around at the group. "I ended up submitting to him because I didn't want to lose the divorce settlement I would get if I hung in there for the next five years." She smiled ruefully at the shocked faced around the circle. "His rules revolved around my being a nicer person and taking better care of myself. I was surprised to find that the threat of spanking actually did influence my behavior. I started to gain weight, started to take classes in domestic sciences and volunteered at a non-profit." She stopped to smile secretively at Stacy.

"After about two weeks it was obvious that Stan wanted something more from me. In my head I was just putting in time until I could leave him…he was trying to mend our marriage." She stopped for a moment and looked down at her hands. "One thing I forgot to mention was that we were ostensibly attempting to get pregnant as well so when Stan came to me with another request, I complied just to keep him happy." A light blush tinged her cheeks as she continued. "He mandated that we do nipple stimulation at least five times a day in order to prepare my breasts for breast feeding. This was a contingency in case we ended up having to adopt a baby." She twisted her hands in her lap. "We started the stimulation immediately. The sessions consisted of Stan sucking on my breasts for at least ten minutes each." She sighed. "Almost right away I noticed that I was very relaxed after each session. Then I started caressing his head while he was on my breast. Later on I began to orgasm from penetration and sucking alone." Bright color now flagged her cheeks. "I started to miss him when he was gone. I anticipated our sessions. Suddenly, I was falling back in love with my husband." She stopped for a moment then started talking again in a soft voice. "The act of offering my body up for my husband's suckling multiple times a day has increased my submission in so many ways." She paused and stared into space. "I will do anything to please him and make him happy now." She indicated her full bosom. "I mean look at them. It isn't easy to carry these around and now that I've started lactating they are even bigger." She absently rubbed the sides of her full breasts. "The only thing that would make me happier right now would be to carry and give birth to his child." Tears stood out in her eyes at these words and her hands dropped into her lap. Stacy and Emily both reached out to hold her hands. The group broke out into applause. When Cecilia looked up, she was surprised to see tears in the eyes of many of the women present. Suddenly she felt more accepted by a group of women than she had in years. She smiled gratefully at Sarah then dropped her head again.

That evening when Stan came home, Cecilia rushed to greet him with a huge kiss. Laughing at her eagerness, he held her back by her arms for a moment. "Not that I'm complaining but why the big kiss?"

She smiled up at him radiantly. "I have new friends. I went to Sarah's Submissive Wives group today and was excited to see some people I know." She stopped for a moment. "Did you know that Stacy and…"

He cut in. "One of the reasons I sent you her way." He kissed the top of her head.

Cecilia's arms wrapped her arms around his waist in a tight hug. "Thank you Stan…for everything."

Tears stood out in her husband's eyes. "No, thank you Darling for your sweet submission." He gently cupped her engorged breasts in his hands. At his touch, Cecilia felt her let down occur and rush out to soak the pads in the bra.

She grabbed Stan's hand to lead him towards the living room. "I need you now. Otherwise, I'm going to have to change into a new dress." She started to pull aside the top of her wrap dress and expertly unlatched one cup of her bra. Stan deftly slipped the button on the top of his pants and freed his cock . Sitting on the couch Stan lifted Cecilia up by her hips and speared her wet cunt on his turgid erection. They both groaned at his penetration. Cecilia desperately held up her tight breast so Stan could start relieving the pressure. With one suck he could feel a little sweet fluid enter his mouth. It tasted so good to him! After Stan latched on, Cecilia started gently working herself on his hard member. Once Stan had relieved the pressure in one swollen orb, he switched to the other one. Cecilia sighed at the sweet relief his mouth offered and her vaginal muscles fluttered on his penis. After Stan finished on the second breast, he grabbed her waist and started working her up and down on his huge cock. He enjoyed the view of her slightly deflated breasts bouncing up and down with his thrusts. Her nipples distended every further than usual from his recent ministrations, dripped small drops of milk as the breasts bounced. It didn't take very long before both of them came. Breathing heavily, they fell together and basked in the afterglow. Stan dropped a hard kiss on her mouth. "I love you Cecee." She smiled at the formerly hated nickname and answered. "I love you too Stan. Forever."

Chapter Eight – The Party

"Once they see how happy you are in a Domestic Discipline relationship, you may find that friends and family will become inspired to try it for themselves." Excerpt from How to Be a Dominant Husband by Penelope Wiggins

 Cecilia looked at her reflection in the full length mirror in the guest suite of her parent's home. Turning around, she examined the tight fitting black sequined dress. Though it was designed to modestly cover her large bosom, it fit her curvaceous body like a glove clear down to her super high, black sequined heels. The earrings and necklace she'd gotten from Stan for Christmas glowed at her neck and ears. She reached up to shift the diamond hair comb the hairdresser had used to accent the elegant up-do he'd created for the benefit party. Damn! She held her hand up in front of her. She'd scratched the nail polish on one of her fingers. Crap! She hadn't brought any nail polish with her. She thought for a moment. Hmmm….Mom probably has a similar color in her collection of polishes. With a mission in mind, Cecilia made her way down the long second floor hallway to the door of her mother's room. Her father's room was right next door. They shared a bathroom. Shaking her head at the thought of sleeping away from Stan, Cecilia knocked gently on her mom's door. No answer. She cracked the door open and let herself into the room. Now where would Mom keep the polish? She started looking around the room. Spotting a tray of polishes on her mom's vanity, Cecilia grabbed one similar to the shade on her own nails.

 As she turned to head back out the door she heard a noise through the doorway to the adjoining bathroom. It sounded like slapping…what the heck? She tip-toed over to open the bathroom door. In the mirror she saw a shocking tableau in her father's bedroom. Her elegantly attired mother was leaning over the back of a chaise longue at the base of the large bed. She was surprised to see that her mother's dress was pulled up to expose her bare buttocks and a bare shaved pussy above the tops of stockings attached to a garter belt. Her mother braced herself with spread out hands on the seat of the chaise. With his back to Cecilia, Quinn wielded a large leather slipper in his hand. While she watched, her father began to spank her mother's ass and thighs with the slipper. Her mother's rear end quickly turned pink then deep red. Cecilia rubbed her own posterior in sympathy. She knew how sore her mom would be for the rest of the night! Her father stopped the spanking and dropped the arm holding the slipper. His Irish lilt floated through the bathroom to Cecilia. "Now that was twenty Helen. Stand up lass." Cecilia's mom stood up sniffling with a red nose. Quinn gently settled himself down on the chaise then pulled a sobbing Helen onto his lap. "Do you understand why I felt the need to give you a whipping before the party tonight?" He gently wiped the tears off of her cheeks with a tissue as he questioned his wife.

Helen rested her head against his chest. She answered between hitching breaths. "So I'll remember to be polite to everyone, even the servants."

Quinn ran a hand up and down Helen's back. "That's right Luv." He kissed the top of her head. "I'm proud of you my brave girl." Cecilia was amazed to see her mother blush and giggle like a school girl then shoot up a flirtatious look at Quinn. Her father's eyes darkened as he looked down at his wife. "I think I'd like a wee sip before the party Darlin'."

Cecilia's jaw dropped when she saw her mother sit up and pull down the wide straps of her ball gown. Underneath the gown her mother wore a utilitarian bra similar to Cecilia's. Her growing suspicions were confirmed when her mother coyly detached a latch on one of the cups and offered her father a large, blue veined breast. The dark nipple jutted up at least one and a half inches. Leaning over to his wife's chest, Quinn expertly latched on and began to suckle industriously. He released the breast with a pop and licked his lips in approval. "Delicious! Now when they say as sweet as mother's milk, I know what they are talking about."

Cecilia's formerly frosty mother blushed and rubbed an affectionate hand on Quinn's cheek. Locking eyes with her husband, she placed the pad on the top of the nipple and re-attached the cup. She matter of factly released the other breast and held it up for her husband. Taking a moment to admire her heavy breasts and elongated nipples, Quinn finally succumbed to her charms and worked the other side. Helen's hands started to roam around his tuxedo clad back and shoulders, occasionally running frantic fingers through his curly black hair. After taking his fill, Quinn released the large orb and looked down at his wife held in his arms. "Do you need a quick fuck now Helen?" Blushing bright red, Helen nodded and climbed off of his lap. "On your knees then on the floor." Quinn ordered. Helen quickly complied leaning down so her forearms were flush to the floor and her skirt was flipped up. Since her back was to Cecilia, Cecilia could see how ready she was for her husband's possession. Slick moisture coated her nether lips right below her bright red ass. Hearing her father's zipper open brought Cecilia out of her fugue state. Shaking her head she crept away from the slightly gapped bathroom door. As she opened the bedroom door, she could hear her mother's long moan.

"Ohhhh Quinn. Fuck me hard!"

Cecilia quickly made her way down the hallway with the forgotten nail polish clutched in her hand. Her cheeks burned at the scene she'd just witnessed. So this was why her parents were getting along so well! She'd also wondered at her mother's larger bosom but hadn't given it much thought. Now it all made sense. She stopped for a moment. Where had they gotten the idea? Had Stan told her father? Oh, how embarrassing! She scurried back to her room and repaired the nail. Sometime later, a knock sounded at the door. "Mrs. Bergstrom, your husband is here in the limousine." Beatty's deep voice came from the other side of the door.

"Okay Beatty. I'll be right down." She answered. She pulled a wrap out of the closet and grabbed a clutch. She kept a hairbrush inside just in case Stan decided that she needed disciplining at the party. She'd learned her lesson the last time she was at the country club! She'd much rather get the hairbrush than her husband's doubled over belt. Running down the front steps of the house, she passed through the front door held open by Beatty and ducked into the limousine. Stan waited for her, looking elegantly handsome in his tux. Not even looking to the front, Cecilia hit the button to close the window between the front and the back of the limousine. "I'm so glad we have this time before the party." She turned around so Stan could unzip her gown. She unlatched one cup of her bra and held the engorged breast up for Stan. He stopped right before latching on.

"I'm sorry that the meeting ran on so late. I really couldn't say no since it was with the bank's CEO."

Cecilia impatiently lifted the heavy orb in her hand and directed the long brown nipple towards his mouth. "I understand, now hurry up so I won't be uncomfortable at the party."

Stan looked at how swollen she was and smiled wryly. "I guess I won't have to eat much tonight at the fundraiser." With these words, he applied himself to providing his wife with some relief. Cecilia felt her stress melt away at his attentions. As he sucked she thought idly about how interdependent they had become. This situation was one of the downsides of their type of relationship. Even when they really didn't want to have a nursing session, they were obligated to do it so she wouldn't be uncomfortable and so she wouldn't leak. She'd had incredible difficulty using a breast pump and it just didn't seem to provide the same relief as her husband. Stan moaned as he worked and she smiled lovingly while stroking his head. When he disengaged and lifted up his head, gazing at her with slumberous eyes. Cecilia suddenly remembered that she wanted to ask him something.

"Stan, did you talk to my dad about our…situation?"

His eyes sharpened and then he nodded sheepishly. "He noticed that you were sore after we'd disappeared at the country club. I had to tell him everything in order to put his mind at ease." He looked at her in askance. "Why do you ask?"

Cecilia blushed. "I accidentally saw him spanking my mom…and then he nursed from her. She actually has milk!"

Stan shook his head. "Wow, that is a pretty short time for her to already be lactating. He must have been sucking on her morning and night!"

Cecilia nodded her head in agreement then looked at the time on the clock in the limousine. "Oh, you need to do the other side. We don't have too much time." She quickly covered the drained breast and uncovered the other swollen orb. Stan quickly set to work and finished up just as they parked in front of the country club. Cecelia raced to make herself presentable right before the valet opened the car door. They triumphantly climbed out of the vehicle and allowed themselves to be ushered up the marble steps to the huge doors leading to the ballroom.

Stacy and her husband Carl stood at the doorway greeting guests. Cecilia had been surprised to learn that Stan's family lived in her home town. They always held the major fundraiser for the Westin Foundation there though Carl and Stacy lived three hours away. Stan placed a proprietary hand at Cecilia's back as he introduced her to Carl. "Westin, this is my wife Cecilia." Shaking Carl's hand, Cecilia felt a shiver as she met his intense dark blue eyes. He bent his raven wing black head over her hand and kissed it gently.

"Enchanted."

Cecilia's wide brown eyes met Stacy's merry blue ones. Sheesh! She'd let him lead her around in a collar and leash any day of the week…uh if she wasn't in love with Stan. Stacy's eyes opened in understanding. Getting over her initial reaction to Carl's magnetism, Cecilia took in her friend's appearance. Used to seeing her blonde friend in jeans and a t-shirt, Cecilia was surprised to see her in a dark blue haute couture gown cupping generous breasts skimming down to reveal the tips of sparkly black high heels. Her gaze swept back up to Stacy's chest. She frowned and looked at Stacy. Was it possible? Stacy nodded her head making the diamond encrusted collar on her neck sparkle. Cecilia finally spoke. "We so have to talk later girlfriend."

Stacy laughed. "You've got a date…I'll talk to you when we're done greeting guests." Stan and Cecilia moved on so the hosts could greet more attendees.

Stan leaned down and whispered in his wife's ear. "So what was that about?"

Cecilia blushed. "I think that Stacy and Carl are…doing what we do. Did you see the size of her chest?"

Stan laughed. "I'll plead the fifth on that one. Let me know if they are. I'd be fine with him giving you relief if we have some sort of emergency where we need to be separated."

Cecilia stopped to look at him in surprise. "Really?"

Stan laid a possessive hand on the back of her neck. "I'm not saying that I'd like it, but at least I know I can trust him."

Cecilia tilted her head. "Would you 'relieve' Stacy in an emergency?"

Stan's lips twisted. "If I had too. You have to understand that it would be a favor to a friend…nothing else. I would want you there the whole time."

Cecilia's shoulders fell in relief. "Okay. Just making sure."

The rest of the evening flew by in a haze with The Westin Foundation making over a million dollars for their various charities. Cecilia saw her friend Emily in passing and frowned at the cleavage bursting over the top of her gown. Another one?

The only dark point in the whole evening was when Cecilia spied Blaine making his way towards her. After she'd unfriended him on Facebook he'd insistently sent numerous e-mails through her private account. She'd finally sent him a terse message asking him to quit contacting her because her husband didn't like it. The e-mails had stopped then. She'd really hoped that he'd gotten the message but her hopes were dashed when he cornered her and started interrogating her about why she'd cut off all contact with him.

"All I can tell you Blaine is that I realized our relationship was not appropriate for me as a married woman. I cut off all contact as a sign of respect to my husband." She looked up earnestly into his face. Studying him close up, she thought he bore an unfortunate resemblance to a pouty baby. His boyish face was bloated and pale. In person he was very unappealing. Cecilia couldn't help but compare him to her sexy husband. She also found it amusing when he looked her up and down and asked her why she'd let herself go. That was the capper for her…what an asshole! She curtly told him to go to hell and flounced away. Later, she'd noticed her husband giving a frightened Blaine a stern talking to. She didn't think he'd be bugging her again anytime soon.

Cecilia smiled when her parents finally made a late entrance into the party. They had their arms wrapped around each other and goofy grins on their faces. They'd never looked happier. She burst out laughing when she saw her Mom's old friend, Blanche, looking at her parents with disgust. Seeing Cecilia's merriment, Blanche turned on her heel and stomped away. This spurred Cecilia on to laugh harder. The old bitch probably got fucked once a year if she was lucky. Cecilia wiped her eyes as a delicate hand grabbed her arm.

"What's so funny?" Stacy inquired.

"Oh, nothing." Cecilia wiped the last bit of tears streaming from her eyes and turned to give her friend a hug. "We need to talk." She led Stacy to a corner. On their way there Cecilia waved Emily down too. All three friends hugged and exclaimed over their gowns. Cecilia looked between them with narrowed eyes. "Okay girls, fess up. What's with the bodacious tatas?" Both women laughed behind their hands.

Emily blushed lightly and glanced over her shoulder at her tall, handsome husband. "When I told Pete about your experience with nipple stimulation he was all over it." The blush crept down to her neck and her bodice. "He now has me submitting to multiple sessions a day. I've already grown two cup sizes. He loves it. As far as he's concerned they can't be too big."

Cecilia cocked her head. "Any milk yet."

Emily shook her head. "Not so far."

Cecilia looked relieved. "Don't rush it. It becomes much more of a responsibility and a potential source of embarrassment when you become engorged and start to leak." She looked rueful. "I should know…we had to do a quick draining session on the way over here." She gave a bark of laughter. "People are going to start to talk. Stan hardly eats anything because he's getting such high calorie nutrients from me. I on the other hand, eat like a stevedore and have difficulty keeping on the weight." She shook her head. She turned her head and looked at Stacy. "Okay girlfriend…fess up."

Stacy rolled her eyes. "I made the mistake of telling Carl about your breastfeeding relationship with Stan. He's such a control freak." She stopped and pink color crept over her cheeks. "No lie, he got an erection when I told him how your breasts have changed since Stan has started sucking on them regularly. I could see the wheels turning in his head for days afterward. He finally came to me and made regular nursing sessions a part of our Master/slave relationship. We are doing it about four times a day. He'd like to expand it to five times but I'm not sure how I can fit that in and work at the daycare. "

Cecilia laid her hand on Stacy's arm. "How about I cover for you while you take a late lunch? That way you could meet him at his office for the fifth session."

Stacy looked at her gratefully. "Thanks Cecee. I really don't like to deny him anything that makes him happy." A warm, loving smile crossed her face as she toyed with the collar around her neck. Looking a little closer, Cecilia noticed a high end dog tag dangling from the collar with the word PET elaborately engraved on it. On the side of the collar she noticed a discrete loop sticking out. Her gaze dropped to the jeweled belt on Stacy's waist. At first glance it was a jeweled belt. On second glance she realized that it was a jeweled leash wrapped twice around her petite waist with the clasp hooked onto the handle. Seeing the direction of Cecilia's gaze, Stacy smiled ruefully. "Yup, I have to wear it on me somewhere at events like this. He'll be leading me around with it later at his favorite BDSM club."

Cecilia looked at her with wide eyes. Yep, Carl was one intense guy. She shivered. She was glad that Stan didn't want her to indulge in any of the more formalized BDSM traditions. She couldn't imagine being on display at a BDSM club. Still…Stacy seemed pretty happy and fulfilled. Hmmm… She shook her head and turned to her friends. "I really need to go find Stan. I have some special news for him later." With a mysterious smile she bid adieu to her friends.

She found Stan laughing and talking with her parents. Slipping a hand into the crook of his elbow, she laid her head on his shoulder. For a moment she basked in parent's happiness. Finally she stood on her tip-toes and whispered in Stan's ear. "I'm ready to go Hon if you are."

He smiled down at her indulgently. "Do you need…?" His eyes moved down to her chest.

She shook her head. "Not yet but soon. I would like to be alone with my husband." Her eyes burned with suppressed passion.

He nodded his head and quickly knocked back the drink in his hand. "Quinn, Helen…we will see you back at the house." Her parents made their goodbyes and the two of them wended their way through the throng of partygoers. The chauffeur quickly drove them back to her parent's house. Cecilia rested her head on Stan's shoulder as he wrapped his arm around her waist. They slowly walked up the steps to their bedroom.

After stripping off their party togs, the couple companionably slipped under the covers in their bed in got into their bedtime suckling position. Cecilia gently played with Stan's hair as he tended to her comfort. Though she held her legs open for him, he seemed content to make this a cuddling session. Releasing her breast with a gently sucking sound he kissed the distended nipple then switched to the other side. Cecilia continued to caress his head. "Stan? I have something to give you when you are done." Stan nodded his head and grunted in understanding as he continued to empty her breast. She could feel his tongue flicking up and pushing under her sensitive nipple. She suddenly found herself overcome with a spontaneous orgasm. Stan obligingly pressed over her mons as she arched against him. The intensity of the release rolled over her and she passed out.

When she came back to her body, her husband hovered over her cupping her cheek. "Cecee are you okay?"

She smiled lovingly. "Yes, the orgasm was so intense I passed out."

He smiled with a bit of pride. "I made you pass out?"

She smacked his shoulder. "Yes, don't act so pleased."

He gathered her close in his arms. "Don't you have something for me?"

Knowing that he was deliberately changing the subject, Cecilia reached into the bedside drawer and presented him with a small rectangular shaped box. A simple ribbon was tied around the box in a bow. Looking at his wife in puzzlement, Stan untied the bow and opened the box. His face turned from curiosity to joy as he lifted up the white stick with a big plus sign on the end. Turning to his wife Stan asked. "Does this mean what I think it means?"

She nodded her head eagerly and pushed herself up to a sitting position. Running her hands down over her abdomen, she cupped the slight roundness right above her pubic bone. "I think that I'm about three months along. I missed a few periods and thought that I was just back to my old pattern. I didn't think much about it until I started feeling a little nauseous in the morning. I did the test this morning and couldn't believe it. We're going to have a baby!"

Stan leaned in and hugged her tight. "Thank you Sweetheart." He buried his head in her neck. Cecilia felt his tears wet her neck. They sat like that for what seemed liked hours then stretched out on the bed together looking into each other's eyes. No words were said as the couple communed silently in the way known to lovers. The eyes, in this case, were truly the window to the soul.

Epilogue- Five Months Later

Stan smiled to himself as he walked through the mudroom to the kitchen in his home. Standing at the stove, stirring a pot of homemade marinara was his very pregnant wife. Her dark brown hair was simply plaited to fall down the middle of her back. Wispy ends teased the sides of her face as the humidity of the food she was cooking made them curl. Her tiny frame, clad in a simple clinging maternity dress, was dwarfed by her massive breasts and stomach. She truly looked like a pagan fertility goddess. His gaze wandered down her body to end up at her bare feet with manicured toes. He smiled at the sight. Walking up behind Cecilia he wrapped his arms around her waist to cup both heavy breasts. "Hello Love." He leaned over to kiss her under a shell-like ear. He continued to whisper in her ear. "Do you remember when you thought that I wanted to put you away on a farm and keep you barefoot and pregnant?" He paused. "Well, two out of three ain't bad." Laughing uncontrollably, he stepped back quickly to dodge the wooden spoon in his wife's hand. So the shrew was still in there somewhere! He chuckled to himself as he took away the spoon and led Cecilia to the living room. Glaring at him, she automatically started unbuttoning her dress. Stan pulled her down on his lap and dropped a laughing kiss on her lips. "I love how you submit to me even when you're mad." Cecilia rolled her eyes and unfastened her bra offering the engorged breast up to him impatiently. Smiling at her ready submission, Stan dropped his lips to the breast. Life was good.

The End

New Novella by Jane Pearl Just Released March 2016!

The Cattle Barons' Submissive
(Discrete Assignments Series Book 3)

-Briana takes a job with Discrete Assignments as a submissive to two sexy Irish brothers in order to make the money to save her family's pub. Her goal is to save the pub and get out of Montana as soon as possible. Unfortunately, the Kerrigan brothers have another idea! 205 pages

Other Novellas and Short Stories by Jane Pearl…

The Cowboys' Submissive (Discrete Assignments Series Book 1)

- Maria took a job with Discrete Assignments in order to escape her homicidal mob boss ex boyfriend. Little did she know that she would end up as the willing submissive to two sexy cowboys! 82 pages

The Submissive School Girl (Discrete Assignments Series Book 2)

- After a bad break-up with her boyfriend, Suzanne decides to take a job with Discrete Assignments in order to pay the bills and get the plastic surgery she thinks she needs to make it big in the movies. She thought her assignment as a submissive to Mr. Bancroft would be a slam dunk. How hard could it be to flounce around in a school girl uniform and maybe give a BJ every once in awhile? Little did she know that Mr. Bancroft wanted much, much more from her…maybe even her heart. 137 pages

The Ranchers' Submissive (Old School Ranchers Series Book 1)

- Pregnant Anna left her husband Cole thirteen years ago because he'd wanted to share her with his brother. Now she needs his help in order to keep their son out of Juvenile Detention. Surprisingly he still wants her back and will let her see their son if she agrees to be a submissive wife to him and his brother Lance! She knows that the two of them will expect total obedience from her in all matters. Will she be able to succumb to their demands without losing herself? 170 pages

The Bull Riders' Submissive (Old School Ranchers Series Book 2)

- After the untimely death of her husband John, Valerie is left to pick up the pieces of her life. Overcome by grief, she gladly accepts the shelter and guidance provided by John's best friend RJ. As she comes out of mourning, she realizes that she has stronger feelings for RJ than friendship. Eventually, with John's blessing, the two of them decide to marry. Though she misses John, Valerie is ecstatic in her new marriage. When RJ suggests that they add a second man to the relationship, Valerie agrees to allow his friend and fellow bull rider Tex Sanchez to court her. While Tex and Valerie explore their relationship, RJ introduces Tex to the tenets of their religion including a belief in domestic discipline! 171 pages

How to Be a Submissive Wife (HTBSW Series Book 1)

- In a last ditch attempt to revive her marriage, Sarah decides to follow the dictates of a book titled, "How to Be a Submissive Wife". Everything ran smoothly until she gave her husband the companion book to hers called, "How to be a Dominant Husband." Little did she know that this book was a Domestic Discipline manual that instructed her husband to set up Rules for her to follow and suggested discipline in the form of spanking if she broke these rules! 62 pages

The Submissive Shrew (HTBSW Series Book 2)

- In an attempt to control his shrewish wife and save his marriage, Stan Bergstrom enforces a Domestic Discipline agreement with the help of a marriage manual written by Penelope Wiggins, the author of How to Be a Submissive Wife. Though their sex life heats up, Stan still wants more emotional intimacy with his wife. On the advice of Ms. Wiggins he implements a last ditch strategy to save his marriage. Though he is skeptical, he attempts to follow Ms. Wiggin's advice to the letter and is surprised at the positive result! 111 pages

The Wives of Brad Masterson – The Honeymoon (TWBM Book 1) and Daisy's Submission (TWBM Book 2)

- Brad Masterson is a large man with large appetites. His first wife Daisy realized early on that there was no way one woman could keep him satisfied. She talked him into adding her younger sister Hyacinth to the marriage. After a few years and a few children the sisters decided that one more wife would be a good idea. They talked their reluctant husband into adding their youngest sister Violet to their marriage. Book 1 is about the Honeymoon with Violet. Book 2 is about is about Daisy's submission to Brad as the head of the household.

This series of short stories is for all of my readers who loved Brad and his Wives in my book The Bull Riders' Submissive. Enjoy!

About Jane Pearl

Ms. Pearl lives in the Pacific Northwest. She is originally from Billings, Montana. She writes erotica that includes themes of Domestic Discipline, Mild BDSM, Spanking, Breast Fetish, Impregnation, Menage, Role Playing, Orgasm Control, Alpha Males and Voyeurism. Though she dabbles in subject matter that might be considered extreme to some, she also creates characters who have humor and heart. Her couples (or trios or more) are loving and committed to each other. If you like strong men and sweet, spunky women you'll love Jane Pearl's novels!

If you have any comments, questions or discussion…please e-mail Jane at JanePearl406@yahoo.com or visit her Facebook Page www.facebook.com/jane/pearl.967

Made in the USA
Columbia, SC
15 February 2025